Doctor Fischer
of Geneva
or the Bomb Party

■

GRAHAM GREENE

SIMON AND SCHUSTER ■ NEW YORK

Copyright © 1980 by Graham Greene
All rights reserved
including the right of reproduction
in whole or in part in any form
Published by Simon and Schuster
A Division of Gulf & Western Corporation
Simon & Schuster Building
Rockefeller Center
1230 Avenue of the Americas
New York, New York 10020
SIMON AND SCHUSTER and colophon
are trademarks of Simon & Schuster
Designed by Edith Fowler
Manufactured in the United States of America

1 2 3 4 5 6 7 8 9 10

Library of Congress Cataloging in Publication Data

Greene, Graham, date.
 Doctor Fischer of Geneva.

 I. Title.
PZ3.G8319Do 1980 [PR6013.R44]
823'.912   80-10314
ISBN 0-671-25467-7
ISBN 0-671-25547-9 deluxe limited ed.

To my daughter, Caroline Bourget,
at whose Christmas table at Jongny
this story first came to me

Who has but once dined his friends
has tasted whatever it is to be Caesar.
                    —HERMAN MELVILLE

Doctor Fischer
of Geneva
or the Bomb Party

1

I think that I used to detest Doctor Fischer more than any other man I have known just as I loved his daughter more than any other woman. What a strange thing that she and I ever came to meet, leave alone to marry. Anna-Luise and her millionaire father inhabited a great white mansion in the classical style by the lakeside at Versoix outside Geneva while I worked as a translator and letter-writer in the immense chocolate factory of glass in Vevey. We might have been a world and not a mere canton apart. I would begin work at 8:30 in the morning while she would be still asleep in her pink and white bedroom, which she told me was like a wedding cake, and when I would go out to eat a hasty sandwich for my lunch, she was probably sitting before her glass in a dressing gown doing her hair. From the sale of their chocolates my employers paid me three thousand francs a month which I suppose may have represented half a morning's unearned income to Doctor Fischer, who many years before had invented Dentophil Bouquet, a toothpaste which was supposed to hold at bay the infections caused by eating too many of our chocolates. The word Bouquet was meant to indicate the choice of perfume, and the first advertisement showed a tasteful bunch of flowers. "Which is your favorite flower?" Later glamorous girls in soft photography would be seen holding between their teeth a flower, which varied with every girl.

But it was not for his money that I detested Doctor Fischer. I hated him for his pride, his contempt of all the world, and his cruelty. He loved no one, not even his daughter. He didn't even bother to oppose our marriage, since he had no greater contempt for me than for his so-called friends who would always flock to him at a nod. Anna-Luise called them "Toads," her English not being perfect. She meant, of course, toadies, but I soon adopted the title which she had given them. Among the Toads was an alcoholic film actor called Richard Deane, a Divisionnaire—a very high rank in the Swiss army, which only has a general in time of war—called Krueger, an international lawyer named Kips, a tax adviser, Monsieur Belmont, and an American woman with blue hair called Mrs. Montgomery. The General, as some of the others called him, was retired, Mrs. Montgomery was satisfactorily widowed, and they all had settled around Geneva for the same reason, either to escape taxes in their own countries or take advantage of favorable cantonal conditions. Doctor Fischer and the Divisionnaire were the only Swiss nationals

in the group when I came to know them and
Fischer was by a long way the richest. He ruled
them all as a man might rule a donkey with a whip
in one hand and a carrot in the other. They were
very well lined themselves, but how they enjoyed
the carrots. It was only for the carrots that they put
up with his abominable parties at which they were
always first humiliated ("Have you no sense of
humor?" I can imagine him demanding at the early
dinners) and then rewarded. In the end they
learned to laugh even before the joke was sprung.
They felt themselves to be a select group—there
were plenty of people around Geneva who envied
them their friendship with the great Doctor
Fischer. (Of what he was a doctor I don't know to
this day. Perhaps they had invented the title to
honor him, just as they called the Divisionnaire
"General.")

How was it that I came to love Fischer's daughter? That needs no explanation. She was young
and pretty, she was warm-hearted and intelligent,
and I cannot think of her now without tears coming to my eyes; but what a mystery must have lain
behind her love for me. She was more than thirty
years younger than I when we met, and there was
certainly nothing about me to attract a girl of her
age. As a young man I had lost my left hand when
I was a fireman in the blitz—that night in December 1940 when the City of London was set ablaze
—and the small pension which I received when the
war was over just enabled me to settle in Switzerland, where the languages that I knew, thanks to

my parents, made it possible for me to make a living. My father had been a minor diplomat, so as a child I had lived in France, Turkey and Paraguay and learned their respective tongues. By a curious coincidence my father and mother were both killed on the same night that I lost my hand; they were buried under the rubble of a house in West Kensington while my hand was left behind somewhere in Leadenhall Street close to the Bank of England.

Like all diplomats my father ended his days as a knight, Sir Frederick Jones—a name which with its dignified prefix no one found comic or unusual in England, though I was to find that a plain Mr. A. Jones was ridiculous in the eyes of Doctor Fischer. Unfortunately for me my father had combined diplomacy with the study of Anglo-Saxon history and, of course with my mother's consent, he gave me the name of Alfred, one of his heroes (I believe she had boggled at Aelfred). This Christian name, for some inexplicable reason, had become corrupted in the eyes of our middle-class world; it belonged exclusively now to the working class and was usually abbreviated to Alf. Perhaps that was why Doctor Fischer, the inventor of Dentophil Bouquet, never called me anything but Jones, even after I married his daughter.

But Anna-Luise—what could have attracted her to a man in his fifties? Perhaps she was seeking a father more sympathetic than Doctor Fischer, just as I may have been unconsciously engaged in a parallel pursuit, of a daughter rather than a wife. My wife had died in childbirth twenty years before, taking with her the child who doctors told me would have been a girl. I was in love with my wife, but I had not reached the age when a man really loves, and perhaps there had not been the time. I doubt if one ever ceases to love, but one can cease to be in love as easily as one can outgrow an author one admired as a boy. The memory of my wife faded quickly enough and it was not constancy which stopped me looking for another wife—to have found one woman who accepted me as a lover in spite of my plastic imitation of a hand and my unattractive income had been a near-miracle, and I couldn't expect a miracle like that to be repeated. When the necessity to have a woman became imperative I could always buy a copulation, even in Switzerland, after I had found my employment in the chocolate factory to augment my pension and the little which I had inherited from my parents (very little it was, but as their capital had been invested in War Loan, at least it paid no English tax).

Anna-Luise and I met first over a couple of sandwiches. I had ordered my usual midday meal, and she was taking a snack before visiting some little woman in Vevey who had been her nurse. I left my table to go to the lavatory while I waited for my sandwich; I had put a newspaper on my chair to keep my place, and Anna-Luise sat herself down on the opposite chair because she hadn't seen the newspaper. When I returned I think she must have noticed my missing hand—in spite of the glove I wore over the plastic substitute—and it was probably for that reason she didn't apologize and move away. (I have already written how kind she was. There was nothing of her father in her. I wish I had known her mother.)

Our sandwiches arrived at the same moment—hers was ham and mine was cheese and she had ordered coffee and I had ordered beer, and there was a moment of confusion with the waitress, who assumed that we were together. . . . And so, quite suddenly, we actually were, like two friends who encounter each other after years of separation. She had hair the color of mahogany with a gloss on it like French polish, long hair which she had pulled up on her scalp and fastened by a shell with a stick through it in what I think is called the Chinese manner, and even while I gave her a polite good morning I was imagining myself pulling out that stick, so that the shell would fall to the floor and her hair down her back. She was so unlike the Swiss girls whom I would see every day in the street, their faces pretty and fresh, all butter and cream, and their eyes blank with an invulnerable lack of experience. She had had experience enough living alone with Doctor Fischer after her mother died.

We exchanged names very quickly before our sandwiches were finished and when she told me "Fischer," I exclaimed, "Not *the* Fischer."

"I wouldn't know who *the* Fischer is."

"Doctor Fischer of the dinners," I said. She nodded and I could see I had given her pain.

"I don't go to them," she said, and I hastened to assure her that rumor always exaggerates.

"No," she said, "the dinners are abominable."

Perhaps it was to change the subject that she then

20

referred directly to my plastic hand over which I always wore a glove to hide the ugliness. Most people pretend not to notice it, though they often take a stealthy look when they think that my attention is elsewhere. I told her of the blitz night in the City of London and how the flames had lit the sky as far away as the West End, so that one could read a book at one in the morning. My station was off the Tottenham Court Road and we were not summoned to help in the east until the early hours. "More than thirty years ago," I said, "but it still seems only a few months away."

"That was the year my father married. What a feast he gave after the ceremony, my mother said. Dentophil Bouquet had already made him a fortune, you see," she added, "and we were neutral and the rich weren't really rationed. I suppose that might count as the first of his dinners. There was French scent for all the women and gold swizzle sticks for the men—he liked to have women at his table in those days. They didn't break up till five in the morning. Not my idea of a wedding night."

"The bombers left us at 5:30," I said. "I was in hospital by then, but I heard the All Clear from my bed." We both ordered another sandwich and she wouldn't let me pay for hers. "Another time," she said, and the words were like the promise of meeting at least once again. The night of the blitz and the sandwich lunch—they are the closest and the clearest memories which I have, clearer even than those of the day when Anna-Luise died.

We finished the sandwiches and I watched her walk out of my sight before I turned toward the office and the five letters in Spanish and the three in Turkish which lay on my desk and were concerned with a new line in milk chocolate flavored with whisky. No doubt Dentophil Bouquet would claim to render it harmless to the gums.

2

So it was that things began for us, but a month of stray meetings in Vevey and of watching classic films in a small cinema in Lausanne halfway between our homes was needed before I realized we were both in love and that she was prepared to "make love" with me, an absurd phrase, for surely we had constructed love a long while before over the ham and cheese sandwiches. We were really a very old-fashioned couple, and I suggested marriage without much hope the first afternoon—it was a Sunday—when I slept with her in the bed I hadn't bothered to make that morning because I had no idea she would consent to come back with me after our rendezvous in the tea shop where we had first met. The way I put it was, "I wish we could be married."

"Why shouldn't we be?" she asked, lying on her back and looking at the ceiling and the shell which the Swiss call the *barrette* lying on the floor and her hair all over the pillow.

"Doctor Fischer," I said. I hated him even before I had met him, and to say "Your father" was repugnant to me, for hadn't she told me that all the rumors about his parties were true?

"We needn't ask him," she said. "Not that I think he'd care anyway."

"I've told you what I earn. It's not much in Swiss terms for two."

"We can manage. My mother left me a little."

"And there's my age," I added. "I'm old enough to be your father," thinking that perhaps I was just that, a substitute for the father she didn't love and that I owed my success to Doctor Fischer. "I could even be your grandfather if I'd started early enough."

She said, "Why not? You're my lover and my father, my child and my mother, you're the whole family—the only family I want," and she put her mouth on mine so that I couldn't reply and she pressed me down onto the bed, so that her blood was smeared on my legs and my stomach, and thus it was we married for better or worse without the consent of Doctor Fischer or a priest if it comes to that. There was no legality in our kind of marriage and therefore there could be no divorce. We took each other for good and all.

She went back to the classical white house by the lake and packed a suitcase (it's amazing how much a woman can get into one case) and came away without a word to anyone. It was only when we had bought a wardrobe and some new things for the kitchen (I hadn't even a frying pan) and a more comfortable mattress for the bed, and perhaps

24

three days had passed, that I said, "He'll wonder where you are." "He"—not "your father."

She was getting her hair right in the Chinese style which I loved. "He may not have noticed," she said.

"Don't you eat together?"

"Oh, he's often out."

"I'd better go and see him."

"Why?"

"He might set the police looking for you."

"They wouldn't look very hard," she said. "I'm above the age of consent. We haven't committed a crime." But all the same I wasn't sure that I had not committed one—a man with only one hand, who was well past fifty, who wrote letters all day about chocolates and who had induced a girl who wasn't yet twenty-one to live with him: not a legal crime of course, but a crime in the eyes of the father. "If you really want to go," she said, "go, but be careful. Please be careful."

"Is he so dangerous?"

"He's hell," she said.

3

I took a day off from work and drove down by the lake, but I very nearly turned back when I saw the extent of the grounds, the silver birches and the weeping willows and the great green cascade of the lawn in front of a pillared portico. A greyhound lay asleep like a heraldic emblem. I felt I should have gone to the tradesmen's entrance.

When I rang the bell a man in a white jacket opened the door. "Doctor Fischer?" I asked.

"What name?" he asked abruptly. I could tell he was English.

"Mr. Jones."

He led me up some stairs into a sort of corridor-lounge with two sofas and several easy chairs and a big chandelier. An elderly woman with blue hair and a blue dress and lots of gold rings occupied one of the sofas. The man in the white jacket disappeared.

We looked at each other, and then I looked at the room, and I thought of the origin of it all—

Dentophil Bouquet. This lounge might have been the waiting room of a very expensive dentist and the two of us sitting there patients. After a while the woman said in English with a faint American accent, "He's such a busy man, isn't he? He has to keep even his friends waiting. I'm Mrs. Montgomery."

"My name is Jones," I said.

"I don't think I've seen you at one of his parties."

"No."

"Of course I sometimes miss one myself. One isn't always around. One can't be, can one? Not always."

"I suppose not."

"Of course you know Richard Deane."

"I've never met him. But I've read about him in the newspapers."

She giggled. "You're a wicked one, I can tell that. You know General Krueger?"

"No."

"But you must know Mr. Kips?" she asked with what seemed like anxiety and incredulity.

"I've heard of him," I said. "He's a tax consultant, isn't he?"

"No, no. That's Monsieur Belmont. How strange that you don't know Mr. Kips."

I felt that some explanation was needed. I said, "I'm a friend of his daughter."

"But Mr. Kips isn't married."

"I meant Doctor Fischer's daughter."

"Oh," she said, "I've never met her. She's very retiring. She doesn't go to Doctor Fischer's parties. Such a pity. We'd all like to know her better."

27

The man in the white jacket returned and said in what sounded to me a rather insolent tone, "Doctor Fischer has a bit of fever, ma'am, and he regrets that he can't receive you."

"Ask him if there's anything he needs—I'll go and get it at once. Some nice muscat grapes?"

"Doctor Fischer has muscat grapes."

"I only meant it as an example. Ask him if there is anything I can do for him, anything at all."

The front door bell rang and the servant, disdaining a reply, went to answer it. He came back up the steps to the lounge followed by a thin old man in a dark suit bowed almost double. He projected his head forward and looked, I thought, rather like the numeral seven. He held his left arm bent at his side, so that he resembled the continental way of writing that number.

"He has a cold," Mrs. Montgomery said, "he won't see us."

"Mr. Kips has an appointment," the manservant said, and taking no more notice of us, he led Mr. Kips up the marble staircase. I called after him, "Tell Doctor Fischer that I have a message from his daughter."

"A bit of fever!" Mrs. Montgomery exclaimed. "Don't you believe it. That's not the way to his bedroom. That's the way to his study. But of course you know the house."

"It's the first time I've been here."

"Oh, I see. That explains it—you're not one of us."

"I'm living with his daughter."

"Really," she said. "How interesting and how

forthright. A pretty girl, I've been told. But I've never seen her. As I said, she doesn't like parties." She put her hand up to her hair, jangling a gold bracelet. "I have all the responsibilities, you see," she said. "I have to act as hostess whenever Doctor Fischer gives a party. I am the only woman he invites nowadays. It's a great honor, of course—but all the same . . . General Krueger generally chooses the wine . . . If there is wine," she added mysteriously. "The General's a great connoisseur."

"Isn't there always wine at his parties?" I asked.

She looked at me in silence as though my question was an impertinent one. Then she relented a little. "Doctor Fischer," she said, "has a great sense of humor. I wonder he hasn't invited you to one of his parties, but perhaps under the circumstances it wouldn't do. We are a *very small* group," she added. "We all know each other well, and we are all so fond, so very, very fond, of Doctor Fischer. But surely you at least know Monsieur Belmont—Monsieur Henri Belmont? He'll solve any tax problem."

"I have no tax problems," I admitted.

As I sat on the second sofa under the great crystal chandelier I realized it was almost as though I had told her that I dropped my h's. Mrs. Montgomery had looked away from me in obvious embarrassment.

In spite of my father's small title which had procured him a niche for a time in *Who's Who* I felt myself an outcast in Mrs. Montgomery's company and now, to add to my shame, the manservant tripped down the stairs and without giving me a glance announced, "Doctor Fischer will see Mr.

Jones at five o'clock on Thursday," and moved away into the unknown regions of the great house which it seemed strange to think had been so recently Anna-Luise's home.

"Well, Mr. Jones, was that the name? It has been pleasant meeting you. I shall stay on awhile to hear from Mr. Kips how our friend fares. We have to look after the dear man."

It was only later that I realized I had encountered the first two Toads.

4

"Give it up," Anna-Luise advised me. "You don't owe him anything. You are not one of the Toads. He knows quite well where I am now."

"He knows you are with someone called Jones—that's all."

"If he wants to he can find out your name, profession, place of business, everything. You are a resident foreigner. The police have your name in the files. He's only got to ask."

"The files are secret."

"Don't believe anything is secret as far as my father is concerned. There's probably a Toad even among the police."

"You make him sound like Our Father in Heaven—his will be done on earth as it is in Heaven."

"That about describes him," she said.

"You make me curious."

"Oh, keep the appointment if you must," she

said. "But be careful. Please be careful. And be more than ever careful if he smiles."

"A Dentophil smile," I mocked her, for indeed both of us used this toothpaste. It had been recommended by my dentist. Perhaps he was a Toad, too.

"Don't ever mention Dentophil to him," she said. "He doesn't like to be reminded of how his fortune was made."

"Doesn't he use it himself?"

"No. He uses a thing called a Water-pik. Keep off the subject of teeth altogether or he'll think you are getting at him. He mocks others, but no one mocks him. He has a monopoly in mockery."

When I cried off work at four o'clock on Thursday I felt none of the courage which I had felt with Anna-Luise. I was just a man called Alfred Jones, earning three thousand francs a month, a man in his fifties, who worked for a chocolate firm. I had left my Fiat with Anna-Luise; I took the train to Geneva and walked from the station to a taxi rank. There was what the Swiss call a Pub Anglais not far from the rank, named, as you would expect, the Winston Churchill, with an unrecognizable sign and wooden paneling and stained-glass windows (for some reason the white and red roses of York and Lancaster) and an English bar with china beer handles, perhaps the only authentic antiques, for that adjective could hardly be applied to the carved wooden settees and the bogus barrels which served as tables and the pressurized Whitbread. The hours of opening I am glad to say were not authentically English and I planned to drink up a little courage before I took a taxi.

As the draft beer was almost as expensive as whisky, I ordered a whisky. I wanted to talk in order to keep my mind off things, so I stood at the bar and tried to engage the landlord in conversation.

"Get many English customers?" I asked.

"No," he said.

"Why? I would have thought . . ."

"They have no money." He was a Swiss and not forthcoming.

I drank a second whisky and went out. I asked the taxi-man, "Do you know Doctor Fischer's house at Versoix?" He was a French Swiss and more forthcoming than the barman.

"Are you going to see the doctor?" he asked.

"Yes."

"You had better be careful."

"Why? He isn't dangerous, is he?"

"*Un peu farfelu,*" he said.

"In what way?"

"You have not heard of his parties?"

"Only rumors. Nobody's ever given me any details."

"Ah, they are sworn to secrecy," he said.

"Who?"

"The people he invites."

"Then how does anybody know about them?"

"Nobody does know," he said.

The same insolent manservant opened the door to me. "Have you an appointment?" he asked.

"Yes."

"What name?"

"Jones."

"I don't know that he can see you."

"I told you, I have an appointment."

"Oh, appointments," he said in a tone of disdain. "Everyone says he has an appointment."

"Run along and tell him I'm here."

He scowled at me and went, leaving me this time on the doorstep. He was quite a long time gone and I nearly walked away. I suspected him of lingering. When at last he returned he said, "He'll see you," and led me through the lounge and up the marble stairs. On the stairs was a painting of a woman in flowing robes holding, with an expression of great tenderness, a skull; I am no expert, but it looked like a genuine seventeenth-century painting and not a copy.

"Mr. Jones," the man announced me.

I looked across the table at Doctor Fischer and was surprised to see a man much like other men (there had been so many hints and warnings), a man more or less of my own age with a red mustache and hair that was beginning to lose its fire— perhaps he tinted the mustache. He had pouches under his eyes and very heavy lids. He looked like a man who didn't sleep well at night. He was seated behind a big desk in the only comfortable chair.

"Sit down, Jones," he said without rising or putting out a hand. It was more of a command than an invitation, yet it was not unfriendly—I might have been one of his employees who was accustomed to stand and to whom he was showing a small favor. I pulled up a chair, and silence fell. At last he said, "You wanted to speak to me?"

"I thought you probably wanted to speak to me."

"How could that be?" he asked. He gave a little smile and I remembered Anna-Luise's warning. "I didn't know you existed until you called the other day. By the way, what does that glove conceal? A deformity?"

"I have lost a hand."

"I imagine you have not come here to consult me about it. I am not that kind of doctor."

"I am living with your daughter. We are thinking of getting married."

"That is always a difficult decision," he said, "but it's one you must take together. It's no affair of mine. Is your deformity a hereditary one? I suppose you will have discussed that important point?"

"I lost it in the London blitz," I said. I added lamely, "We thought you should be told."

"Your hand hardly concerns me."

"I meant about our marriage."

"That information could have been conveyed, I would have thought, more easily in writing. It would have saved you a journey to Geneva." He made Geneva sound as distant socially from our home in Vevey as Moscow.

"You don't seem very concerned about your daughter."

"You probably know her better than I do, Jones, if you know her well enough to marry her, and you have relieved me of any responsibility I may once have had."

"Don't you want to have her address?"

35

"I imagine she lives with you?"

"Yes."

"I suppose you are in the telephone book?"

"Yes. Under Vevey."

"Then there's no need for you to write the address down." He gave me another of his little dangerous smiles. "Well, Jones, it was polite of you to have called, even if it was not really necessary." It was obviously a dismissal.

"Good-bye, Doctor Fischer," I said. I had nearly reached the door when he spoke again.

"Jones," he said, "do you happen to know anything about porridge? Real porridge I mean. Not Quaker oats. Perhaps being Welsh—you have a Welsh name—"

"Porridge is a Scottish dish," I said, "not Welsh."

"Ah, I have been misinformed. Thank you, Jones. That is all, I think."

When I got home Anna-Luise greeted me with an anxious face. "How did you get on?"

"I didn't get on at all."

"He was a beast to you?"

"I wouldn't say that—he was totally uninterested in both of us."

"Did he smile?"

"Yes."

"He didn't invite you to a party?"

"No."

"Thank God for that."

"Thank Doctor Fischer," I said, "or is it the same thing?"

5

A week or two later we got married at the *Mairie* with a witness whom I brought from the office. There had been no communication from Doctor Fischer, although we had sent him an announcement of the date. We felt very happy, all the more happy because we would be alone—except, of course, for the witness. We made love half an hour before we went to the *Mairie*. "No cake," Anna-Luise said, "no bridesmaids, no priest, no family—it's perfect. This way it's solemn—one feels really married. The other way is like a party."

"One of Doctor Fischer's parties?"

"Almost as bad."

There was someone standing at the back of the room in the *Mairie* whom I didn't know. I had looked nervously over my shoulder, because I half-expected the arrival of Doctor Fischer, and saw a very tall lean man with hollow cheeks and a

twitch in his left eyelid which made me think for a
moment that he was winking at me, but, as he gave
me a blank glare when I winked back, I assumed
he was an official, attached to the mayor. Two
chairs had been placed for us in front of the table,
and the witness, called Monsieur Excoffier, hov-
ered nervously behind us. Anna-Luise whispered
something I didn't catch.

"What did you say?"

"He's one of the Toads."

"Monsieur Excoffier!" I exclaimed.

"No, no, the man at the back." Then the ceremony began, and I felt nervous all through the
affair, because of the man behind us. I remembered the place in the Anglican service where the
clergyman asks if there is anyone who knows just
cause or impediment why these two persons should
not be joined in Holy Matrimony you are to declare
it, and I couldn't help wondering whether a Toad
mightn't have been sent for that very purpose by
Doctor Fischer. However, the question was never
asked, nothing happened, everything went
smoothly, and the mayor—I suppose it was the
mayor—shook our hands and wished us happiness
and then disappeared quickly through a door behind the table. "Now for a drink," I said to Monsieur Excoffier—it was the least we could do in
return for his mute services—"a bottle of champagne at the Trois Couronnes."

But the thin man still stood there winking at us
from the back of the room. "Is there another way
out?" I asked the clerk of the court—if that is what

he was—and I indicated the door behind the table, but no, he said no. It was quite impossible for us to go that way—that wasn't for the public, so there was nothing we could do but face the Toad. When we reached the door the stranger stopped me. "Monsieur Jones, my name is Monsieur Belmont. I have brought something for you from Doctor Fischer." He held out an envelope.

"Don't take it," Anna-Luise said. We both in our ignorance thought it might be a writ.

"Madame Jones, he has sent his best wishes for your happiness."

"You are a tax adviser, aren't you?" she said. "What are his best wishes worth? Do I have to declare them to the *fisc?*"

I had opened the envelope. There was only a printed card inside. "Doctor Fischer requests the pleasure of the company of . . ." (he had filled in the name Jones without so much as a Mister) "at a reunion of his friends and an informal dinner on . . ." (he had written in "November 10") "at 8:30 P.M. R.S.V.P."

"It's an invitation?" Anna-Luise asked.

"Yes."

"You mustn't go."

"He will be very disappointed," Monsieur Belmont said. "He particularly hopes that Monsieur Jones will come and join us all. Madame Montgomery will be there and of course Monsieur Kips and we hope that the Divisionnaire . . ."

"A gathering of the Toads," Anna-Luise said.

"Toads? Toads? I do not know the word. Please,

he wishes very much to introduce your husband to all his friends."

"But I see from the card that my wife is not invited."

"None of our wives are invited. No ladies. It has become a rule for our little gatherings. I do not know why. There was once . . . but Madame Montgomery is the only exception now. You might say that in herself she is the representative of her sex." He added a piece of unfortunate slang, "She's a good sort."

"I will send a reply this evening," I said.

"You will miss a great deal, I assure you, if you do not come. Doctor Fischer's parties are always very entertaining. He has a great sense of humor, and he is so generous. We have much fun."

We drank our bottle of champagne with Monsieur Excoffier at the Trois Couronnes and then we went home. The champagne was excellent, but the sparkle had gone out of the day. Doctor Fischer had introduced a conflict between us, for I began to argue that after all I had nothing really against Doctor Fischer. He could easily have opposed our marriage or at least expressed disapproval. By sending me an invitation to one of his parties he had in a sense given me a wedding present which it would be churlish to refuse.

"He wants you to join the Toads."

"But I've got nothing against the Toads. Are they really as bad as you say? I've seen three of them. I admit I didn't much care for Mrs. Montgomery."

"They weren't always Toads, I suppose. He's corrupted all of them."

"A man can only be corrupted if he's corruptible."

"And how do you know you aren't?"

"I don't. Perhaps it's a good thing to find out."

"So you'll let him take you into a high place and show you all the kingdoms of the world."

"I'm not Christ, and he's not Satan, and I thought we'd agreed he was God Almighty, although I suppose to the damned God Almighty looks very like Satan."

"Oh, all right," she said, "go and be damned."

The quarrel was like a dying wood fire: sometimes it seemed to dwindle out, but then a gathering of sparks would light a splinter of charred wood and flare for a moment into a flame. The dispute only ended when she wept against the pillow and I surrendered. "You're right," I said, "I don't owe him anything. A piece of pasteboard. I won't go. I promise I won't go."

"No," she said, "you are right. I'm wrong. I know you aren't a Toad, but *you* won't know you aren't unless you go to that damned party. Please go. I'm not angry anymore, I promise. I want you to go." She added, "After all, he *is* my father. Perhaps he's not all that bad. Perhaps he'll spare you. He didn't spare my mother."

We were tired out by the dispute. She fell asleep in my arms without making love, and presently I slept too.

Next morning I sent my formal reply to the invitation: "Mr. A. Jones has pleasure in accepting Dr. Fischer's kind invitation . . ." I couldn't help saying to myself: What a fuss about nothing, but I was wrong, quite wrong.

6

The quarrel was not revived. That was one of the great qualities of Anna-Luise: she never went back to a quarrel or back on an agreed decision. I knew, when she decided to marry me, she meant it to be for life. She never once mentioned the party again and the next ten days were among the happiest I've ever spent. It was an extraordinary change for me to come home at night from the office to a flat which wasn't empty and to the sound of a voice which I loved.

On one occasion only the happiness seemed a little threatened when I had to go into Geneva to see an important Spanish confectioner from Madrid on some business for the firm. He gave me an excellent lunch at the Beau Rivage, but I couldn't take full advantage of the meal because he talked about nothing but chocolate from our *apéritifs* on —I remember he chose an Alexander cocktail sprinkled with grains of chocolate. You might think the subject of chocolate a rather limited one, but it certainly wasn't, not to an important confectioner with revolutionary ideas. He finished the meal with a chocolate mousse, which he criticized severely because it didn't contain some scraps of orange skin. When I left I felt a bit liverish, as though I had sampled every kind of chocolate my firm had ever manufactured.

It was a heavy humid autumn day and I walked away toward the place where I had left my car, trying to escape the wetness of the air and the wetness of the lake and the taste of chocolate which clotted my tongue, when a woman's voice said, "Why, Mr. Smith, you are exactly the man I want." I turned and there was Mrs. Montgomery in the doorway of an expensive shop—a kind of Swiss Asprey's.

I said, "Jones," automatically.

"I'm so sorry. Oh, what a memory I have. I don't know why I thought you were Mr. Smith. But it doesn't make any difference because it's a man I want. Just a man. That's all."

"Is this a proposition?" I asked, but she didn't see the joke.

She said, "I want you to come in here and point out four objects which you would like to possess— if you were extravagant enough to buy them."

She pulled me into the shop by the arm and the sight of all those luxury goods sickened me rather as the chocolate at lunch had done—everything seemed to be in gold (eighteen karat) or platinum, although for the poorer customers there were objects in silver and pigskin. I remembered the rumors which I had heard about Doctor Fischer's parties, and I thought I knew what Mrs. Montgomery was after. She picked up a red morocco case containing a gold cigar cutter. "Wouldn't you like to have this?" she asked. It would have cost me nearly a month's salary.

"I don't smoke cigars," I said. I added, "You shouldn't choose that. Didn't he give those away at his wedding party? I don't suppose Doctor Fischer likes repeating himself."

"Are you sure?"

"No. I think after all they were swizzle sticks."

"But you aren't *sure?*" she asked in a tone of disappointment and put the cigar cutter down. "You don't know how difficult it is to find something which will please everybody—especially the men."

"Why not just give them checks?" I asked.

"You can't give checks to people. It would be insulting."

"Perhaps none of you would be insulted if the checks were large enough."

I could see she was reflecting on what I said, and I have reason to believe from what happened later that she must have repeated my remark to Doctor Fischer. She said, "It wouldn't do. It wouldn't do at all. Think of giving a check to the General—it would look like a bribe."

"Generals have taken bribes before now. Anyway, he can't be a general if he's Swiss. He's probably only a Divisionnaire."

"But the idea of giving a check to Mr. Kips. Why, it's unthinkable. You mustn't tell anyone I told you, but Mr. Kips in fact owns this store." She brooded. "What about a quartz watch in gold—or better still, platinum? But then perhaps they have one already."

"They could always sell the new one back."

"I'm sure not one of them would dream of selling a gift. Not a gift from Doctor Fischer."

So my guess proved to be right and the secret was out. I saw her gulp as though she were trying to swallow it back.

I picked up a pigskin photograph frame. As though people who shopped in that store mightn't be clever enough to know what one used a pigskin photograph frame for, the management had inserted a photograph of Richard Deane, the film star. Even I had read enough newspapers to recognize that handsome old-young face and the alcoholic smile.

"What about this?" I asked.

"Oh, you're impossible," Mrs. Montgomery wailed, but all the same, as it turned out, she must have repeated even that mocking suggestion back to Doctor Fischer.

I think she was glad to see me go. I hadn't been helpful.

7

"Do you hate your father?" I asked Anna-Luise
after I had told her all the events of that day, beginning with my lunch with the Spanish confectioner.

"I don't like him." She added, "Yes, I think I do
hate him."

"Why?"

"He made my mother miserable."

"How?"

"It was his pride. His infernal pride." She told
me how her mother loved music, which her father
hated—there was no doubt at all of *that* hatred.
Why it was she had no idea, but it was as if music
taunted him with his failure to understand it, with
his stupidity. Stupid? The man who had invented
Dentophil Bouquet and founded a fortune of
many million francs stupid? So her mother began
to slip away to concerts on her own and at one of
them she met a man who shared her love of music.
They even bought discs and listened to them in
secret in his flat. When Doctor Fischer talked of the

caterwauling of the strings she no longer tried to argue with him—she had only to walk down a street near the butcher's, speak in a parlophone and take a lift to the third floor and listen for an hour happily to Heifetz. There was no sex between them—Anna-Luise was sure of that, it was not a question of fidelity. Sex was Doctor Fischer, and her mother had never enjoyed it: sex was the pain of childbirth and a great sense of loneliness when Doctor Fischer grunted with pleasure. For years she had pretended pleasure herself: it wasn't difficult to deceive him since her husband was not interested in whether she had pleasure or not. She might well have saved herself the trouble. All this she had told her daughter in one hysterical outburst.

Then Doctor Fischer had discovered what she was about. He questioned her and she told him the truth, and he didn't believe the truth—or perhaps he did believe, but it made no difference to him whether she was betraying him with a man or with a record of Heifetz, a record of all that caterwauling he couldn't understand. She was leaving him by entering a region into which he couldn't follow her. His jealousy so infected her that she began to feel he must have a reason for it—she felt herself guilty of something, though of what she wasn't sure. She apologized, she abased herself, she told him everything—even which record of Heifetz pleased her most, and ever after it seemed to her that he made love with hatred. She couldn't explain that to her daughter, but I could imagine the way it went—how he thrust his way in, as though he were stabbing an enemy. But he couldn't be satisfied with one final blow. It had to be the death of a thousand cuts. He told her he forgave her, which only increased her sense of guilt, for surely there had to be something to forgive, but he told her also that he could never forget her betrayal—what betrayal? So he would wake her in the night to stab her with his goad again. She learned that he had discovered the name of her friend—that harmless little lover of music—and he went to the man's employer and gave him fifty thousand francs to sack him without a reference. "That was Mr. Kips," she said. Her friend was only a clerk—he wasn't important—he was no better than a clone that you could replace with another clone. His only distinguishing feature had been his love of music, and Mr. Kips knew nothing of that. To Doctor Fischer it was an added humiliation that the man earned so little. He wouldn't have minded being betrayed by another millionaire—or so her mother believed. He would certainly have despised Christ for being the son of a carpenter, if the New Testament had not proved in time to be such a howling commercial success.

"What happened to the man?"

"My mother never knew," Anna-Luise said. "He simply disappeared. And my mother disappeared too after a few years. I think she was like an African who can just will herself to die. She only spoke to me once about her private life, and that's what I've told you. As I remember it."

"And you? How did he treat you?"

"He never treated me badly. He wasn't interested in me enough for that. But do you know, I

49

think the little clerk of Mr. Kips had really pricked him to the heart, and he never recovered from the prick. Perhaps it was then he learned how to hate and to despise people. So the Toads were summoned to amuse him after my mother died. Mr. Kips, of course, was the first of them. He couldn't have been happy about Mr. Kips. He had in a way exposed himself to Mr. Kips. So he had to humiliate him like he humiliated my mother, because Mr. Kips knew. He made him his lawyer, because that shut his mouth."

"But what did he do to Mr. Kips?"

"Of course you don't know what Mr. Kips looks like."

"I do. I saw him when I tried to see your father the first time."

"Then you know he's bent almost double. Something wrong with his spine."

"Yes. I thought he looked like the number seven."

"He hired a well-known writer for children and a very good cartoonist and between them they produced a kind of strip-cartoon book called *The Adventures of Mr. Kips in Search of a Dollar.* He gave me an advance copy. I didn't know there was a real Mr. Kips and I found the book very funny and very cruel. Mr. Kips in the book was always bent double and always seeing coins people had dropped on the pavement. It was the Christmas season when the book appeared and my father arranged—for money of course—a big display in every bookshop window. The display had to be at a certain height, so that Mr. Kips bent double could see if he passed that way. A lawyer's name—especially an international lawyer who doesn't deal in popular things like crime—is never very well known, even in the city where he lives, and I think only one bookshop objected for fear of libel. My father simply guaranteed to pay any costs. The book—I suppose most children are cruel—became a popular success. There were many reprints. There was even a strip cartoon in a newspaper. I believe my father—and that must have given him great pleasure—made a lot of money out of it."

"And Mr. Kips?"

"The first he knew about it was at the first of my father's special dinners. Everyone had a small and magnificent present—something in gold or platinum—beside his plate, except Mr. Kips, who had a big brown paper parcel containing a specially bound copy of the book in red morocco. He must have been furious, but he had to pretend to be amused before the other guests, and anyway he could do nothing because my father was paying him a very large retaining fee for which he did nothing at all and which he would lose if there was a quarrel. Who knows? Perhaps it was he who bought up so many copies that the book became a success. My father told me all about it. He thought the story was very funny. 'But why poor Mr. Kips?' I asked. Of course he didn't tell me the real reason. 'Oh, I'll have fun with all of them in time,' he told me. 'Then you'll lose all your friends in time,' I said. 'Don't you believe it,' he said. 'All my friends are rich, and the rich are the greediest. The rich have no pride except in their possessions. You only have to be careful with the poor.' "

"Then we are safe," I said. "We aren't rich."

"Yes, but perhaps we aren't poor enough for him."

She had a wisdom which I couldn't match. Perhaps that was another of the reasons why I loved her.

8

Now that I'm alone in this flat I try to remember the happiness we shared before that first party with the Toads. But how does one convey happiness? Unhappiness we can so easily describe—I was unhappy, we say, because . . . We remember this and that, giving good reasons, but happiness is like one of those islands far out in the Pacific which has been reported by sailors when it emerges from the haze where no cartographer has ever marked it. The island disappears again for a generation, but no navigator can be quite certain that it only existed in the imagination of some long-dead lookout. I tell myself over and over again how happy I was in those weeks, but when I search my head for the reason I can find nothing adequate to explain my happiness.

Is there happiness in a sexual embrace? Surely not. That is an excitement, a kind of delirium, and sometimes it is close to pain. Is happiness simply the sound of a quiet breath on the pillow beside me, or kitchen noises in the evening when I returned from work and read the *Journal de Genève* in our only easy chair? We could have well afforded a second chair, but somehow we never had the time to find one in those weeks, and when finally we bought it in Vevey—and a dishwasher too which substituted the noise of an engine room for the cheerful clangor of a human washing-up—the island of great happiness had been lost already in the haze.

The approaching menace of Doctor Fischer's party had come between us by that time and it filled our silences. A darker shadow than an angel passed over our heads. Once at the end of some such long pause I spoke my thought aloud: "I think I'll write to him after all and tell him I can't come. I'll say . . ."

"What?"

"We are taking a holiday, I'll say—on the only date the firm will allow me."

"People don't take holidays in November."

"Then I'll write that you are not well and I can't leave you."

"He knows that I'm as strong as a horse."

And that in a way was true, but the horse must have been a thoroughbred, which I believe always needs a great deal of care. She was slim and fine-boned. I liked to touch her cheekbones and the curve of her skull. Her strength showed mainly in her small wrists, which were as strong as whipcord: she could always open a screw jar which foxed me.

"Better not," she said. "You were right to accept and I was wrong. If you call it off now, you will think you are a coward and never forgive yourself. After all, it's only one party. He can't hurt us really. You aren't Mr. Kips and you aren't rich and we don't depend on him. You need never go to another."

"I certainly won't," I said and I believed it. All the same, the date was approaching fast. A great cloud lay over the sea, the island had gone from sight and I should never know the latitude and longitude to mark it on any map. The time would come when I would doubt if I had ever really seen the island.

There was something else we bought in that bout of shopping, and that was a pair of skis. Her mother had taught Anna-Luise to ski when she was four years old, so that to ski was as natural to her as to walk, and the season of snow was approaching. When she joined me in Vevey she had left her skis at home and nothing would induce her to return and fetch them. . . . And there were boots, too, to find. It proved a long shopping day and we were still, I suppose, quite happy; as long as we were occupied we had no eye for clouds. I liked watching her expertise when she chose her skis, and her feet had never seemed prettier than when she was trying on the heavy boots she needed.

Coincidences in my experience are seldom happy. How hypocritically we say "What a happy coincidence!" when we meet an acquaintance in a strange hotel where we want very much to be alone. We passed a *librairie* on our way home, and I always look in the window of any bookshop—it is almost an automatic reflex. In this one there was a

55

window full of children's books, for in November the shops are already preparing for the Christmas trade. I took my automatic glance, and there in the very center of the window was Mr. Kips, head bent to the pavement, in search of a dollar.

"Look."

"Yes," Anna-Luise said, "there's always a new edition in time for Christmas. Perhaps my father pays the publisher or perhaps there are always new children to read it."

"Mr. Kips must wish the pill was universally used."

"When the skiing's over," Anna-Luise said, "I'm going to drop the pill myself. So perhaps there'll be another reader of Mr. Kips."

"Why wait till then?"

"I'm a good skier," she said, "but there are always accidents. I don't want to be pregnant in plaster."

We couldn't avoid the thought of Doctor Fischer's party any longer. "Tomorrow" had almost arrived and was already there in both our minds. It was as though a shark were nuzzling beside our small boat, from which we had once seen the island. We lay awake in bed for hours that night, a shoulder touching a shoulder, but we were separated an almost infinite distance by our distress.

"How absurd we are," Anna-Luise argued, "what on earth can he do to us? You aren't Mr. Kips. Why, he could fill all the shops with a caricature of your face and what would we care? Who would recognize you? And your firm isn't going to sack you because he pays them fifty thousand francs.

That's not half an hour's income to them. We don't depend on him for anything. We are free, free. Say it aloud after me. Free."

"Perhaps he hates freedom as much as he despises people."

"There's no way he can turn you into a Toad."

"I wish I knew why he wants me there then."

"It's just to show the others that he can get you to come. He may try to humiliate you in front of them—it would be like him. Bear it for an hour or two, and, if he goes too far, fling your wine in his face and walk out. Always remember we are free. Free, darling. He can't hurt you or me. We are too little to be humiliated. It's like when a man tries to humiliate a waiter—he only humiliates himself."

"Yes, I know. Of course you are right. It *is* absurd, but all the same I wish I knew what he had in mind."

We went to sleep at last and the next day moved as slowly as a cripple, like Mr. Kips, toward the evening hour. The very secrecy in which Doctor Fischer's dinners had been held, and the spate of unlikely rumors, made them sinister, but surely the presence of the same group of Toads must mean there was some entertainment to be found in them. Why did Mr. Kips ever attend again after he had been so insulted? Well, perhaps that could be explained by his unwillingness to lose his retaining fee, but the Divisionnaire—surely he would not put up with anything really disgraceful? It isn't easy to reach the rank of Divisionnaire in neutral Switzerland, and a Divisionnaire, a retired Divisionnaire, has the prestige of a rare and protected bird.

I remember every detail of that uneasy day. The toast at breakfast was burned—it was my fault; I arrived at the office five minutes late; two letters in Portuguese were sent me to translate, although I knew no Portuguese; I had to work through lunchtime thanks to the Spanish confectioner who, encouraged by our lunch together, had sent in twenty pages of suggestions and demanded a reply before he returned to Madrid (among other things he wanted a modification of one of our lines to suit Basque taste—it seemed in some way that I didn't understand, we were underestimating the strength of Basque national feeling in our milk chocolates flavored with whisky). I was very late in getting home and I cut myself shaving and nearly put on the wrong jacket with my only pair of dark trousers. I had to stop at a petrol station on the way to Geneva and pay cash because I had forgotten to transfer my credit card from one suit to another. All these things appeared to me like omens of an unpleasant evening.

9

The disagreeable manservant, whom I had hoped never to see again, opened the door. There were five expensive cars lounging in the drive, two of them with chauffeurs, and I thought that he looked at my little Fiat 500 with disdain. Then he looked at my suit and I could see that his eyebrows went up. "What name?" he asked, though I felt sure he remembered it well enough. He spoke in English with a bit of a cockney twang. So he had remembered my nationality.

"Jones," I said.

"Doctor Fischer's engaged."

"He's expecting me," I said.

"Doctor Fischer's dining with friends."

"I happen to be dining with him myself."

"Have you an invitation?"

"Of course I have an invitation."

"Let me see the card."

"You can't. I left it at home."

He scowled at me, but he wasn't confident—I

could tell that. I said, "I don't think Doctor Fischer would be very pleased if there's an empty place at his table. You'd better go and ask him."

"What did you say your name was?"

"Jones."

"Follow me."

I followed his white coat through the hall and up the stairs. On the landing he turned to me. He said, "If you've been lying to me . . . If you weren't invited . . ." He made a motion with his fists like a boxer sparring.

"What's your name?" I asked.

"What's that to do with you?"

"I just want to tell the Doctor how you welcome his friends."

"Friends," he said. "He has no friends. I tell you, if you weren't invited . . ."

"I am invited."

We turned the opposite way from the study where I had last seen Doctor Fischer and he flung open a door. "Mr. Jones," the man grunted and I walked in, and there stood all the Toads looking at me. The men wore dinner jackets and Mrs. Montgomery a long dress.

"Come in, Jones," Doctor Fischer said. "You can serve dinner as soon as it's ready, Albert."

The table was laid with crystal glasses which caught the lights of a chandelier overhead: even the soup plates looked expensive. I wondered a little at seeing them there: it was hardly the season for cold soup. "This is Jones, my son-in-law," Doctor Fischer said. "You must excuse his glove. It

60

covers a deformity. Mrs. Montgomery, Mr. Kips, Monsieur Belmont, Mr. Richard Deane, Division-naire Krueger." (Not for him to mistitle Krueger.) I could feel the fumes of their hostility projected at me like tear gas. Why? Perhaps it was my dark suit. I had lowered what apartment builders would call the "standing."

"I have met Monsieur Jones," Belmont said as though he were a prosecution witness identifying the accused.

"Me too," said Mrs. Montgomery, "briefly."

"Jones is a great linguist," Doctor Fischer said. "He translates letters about chocolates," and I realized he must have made inquiries about me from my employers. "Here, Jones, at our little parties we use English as our common language because Richard Deane, great star though he may be, speaks no other, though he sometimes attempts a kind of French in his cups—after his third one. On the screen you've only heard him dubbed in French."

Everyone laughed as though on cue except Deane, who gave a mirthless smile. "He has the qualities after a drink or two to play Falstaff except a lack of humor and a lack of weight. The second tonight we shall do our best to remedy. The humor, I'm afraid, is beyond us. You may ask what is left. Only his fast-diminishing reputation among women and teenagers. Kips, you are not enjoying yourself. Is something wrong? Perhaps you miss our usual *apéritifs*, but tonight I didn't want to spoil your palates for what's coming."

"No, no, I assure you nothing is wrong, Doctor Fischer. Nothing."

"I always insist," Doctor Fischer said, "at my little parties that everybody enjoys himself."

"They are a riot," Mrs. Montgomery said, "a riot."

"Doctor Fischer is invariably a very good host," Divisionnaire Krueger informed me with condescension.

"And so generous," Mrs. Montgomery said. "This necklace I'm wearing—it was a prize at our last party." She was wearing a heavy necklace of gold pieces—they seemed to me from a distance to be Krugerrands.

"There is always a little prize for everyone," the Divisionnaire murmured. He was certainly old and gray and he was probably full of sleep. I liked him the best because he seemed to have accepted me more easily than the others.

"There the prizes are," Mrs. Montgomery said. "I helped him choose." She went over to a side table where I noticed now a pile of gift-wrapped parcels. She touched one with the tip of a finger like a child testing a Christmas stocking to tell from the crackle what is within.

"Prizes for what?" I asked.

"Certainly not for intelligence," Doctor Fischer said, "or the Divisionnaire would never win anything."

Everyone was watching the pile of gifts.

"All we have to do is just to put up with his little whims," Mrs. Montgomery explained, "and then he distributes the prizes. There was one evening—

can you believe it?—he served up live lobsters with bowls of boiling water. We had to catch and cook our own. One lobster nipped the General's finger."

"I bear the scar still," Divisionnaire Krueger complained.

"The only wound in action which he has ever received," Doctor Fischer said.

"It was a riot," Mrs. Montgomery told me as though I might not have caught the point.

"Anyway it turned her hair blue," Doctor Fischer said. "Before that night it was an unsavory gray stained with nicotine."

"Not gray—a natural blond—and not nicotine-stained."

"Remember the rules, Mrs. Montgomery," Doctor Fischer said. "If you contradict me once again you will lose your prize."

"That happened once at one of our parties to Mr. Kips," Monsieur Belmont said. "He lost an eighteen-karat gold lighter. Like this one." He took a leather case from his pocket.

"It was little loss to me," Mr. Kips said. "I don't smoke."

"Be careful, Kips. Don't denigrate my gifts—or yours might disappear a second time tonight."

I thought: But surely this is a madhouse ruled by a mad doctor. It was only curiosity which kept me there—certainly it was not for any prize that I stayed.

"Perhaps," Doctor Fischer said, "before we sit down to dinner—a dinner I very much hope that you'll enjoy and do full justice to, as I have given a great deal of thought to the menu—I should explain to our new guest the etiquette we observe at these dinners."

"Most necessary," Belmont said. "I think—if you will excuse me—you should perhaps have put his appearance here—shall we say?—to the vote? After all, we are a kind of club."

Mr. Kips said, "I agree with Belmont. We all of us know where we stand. We accept certain conditions. It's all in the spirit of fun. A stranger might misunderstand."

"Mr. Kips in search of a dollar," Doctor Fischer said. "You are afraid that the value of the prizes may be reduced with another guest just as you hoped the value would rise after the death of two of our number."

There was a silence. I thought from the expression in his eyes that Mr. Kips was about to make an angry reply, but he didn't: all he said was, "You misunderstand me."

Now all of this, read by someone not present at the party, might well sound no more than the jolly banter of clubmen who insult each other in a hearty way before sitting down to a good dinner and some heavy drinking and good companionship. But to me, as I watched the faces and detected how near the knuckle the teasing seemed to go, there was a hollowness and a hypocrisy in the humorous exchanges and hate like a rain cloud hung over the room—hatred of his guests on the part of the host and hatred of the host on the part of the guests. I felt a complete outsider, for though I disliked every one of them, my emotion was too weak as yet to be called hatred.

"To the table then," Doctor Fischer said, "and I will explain to our new guest the purpose of my little parties, while Albert brings in the dinner."

I found myself sitting next to Mrs. Montgomery, who was on the right of the host. I had Belmont on my right and the actor Richard Deane opposite me. Beside every plate was a bottle of good Yvorne, except beside our host's, who, I noticed, preferred Polish vodka.

"First," Doctor Fischer said, "I would ask you to toast the memory of our two—friends shall I call them on this occasion?—on the anniversary of their deaths two years ago. An odd coincidence. I chose the date for that reason. Madame Faverjon died by her own hand. I suppose she could no longer stomach herself—it was difficult enough for me to stomach her, though I had found her at first an interesting study. Of all the people at this table she was the greediest—and that is saying a good deal. She was also the richest of all of you. There have been moments when I have watched each one of you show a sign of rebelling against the criticisms I have made of you and I have been forced to remind you of the presents at the end of dinner, which you were in danger of forfeiting. That was never the case with Madame Faverjon. She accepted everything and anything in order to qualify for her present, though she could easily have afforded to buy one of equal value for herself. She was an abominable woman, an unspeakable woman, and yet I had to admit she showed a certain courage at the end. I doubt if one of you would ever show as much, not even our gallant Division-

naire. I doubt if one of you has even contemplated ridding the world of his unnecessary presence. So I'll ask you to toast the ghost of Madame Faverjon."

I obeyed like all the others.

Albert entered carrying a silver tray on which there was a large pot of caviar and little silver dishes of egg and onion and sliced lemons.

"You will excuse Albert for serving me first," Doctor Fischer said.

"I adore caviar," Mrs. Montgomery said. "I could live on it."

"You could afford to live on it if you were prepared to spend your own money."

"I'm not such a rich woman as all that."

"Why bother to lie to me? If you weren't as rich as you are you would not be sitting at this table. I invite only the very rich."

"What about Mr. Jones?"

"He is here as an observer rather than as a guest, but of course, as he is my son-in-law, he may imagine he has great expectations. Expectations too are a form of wealth. I am sure Mr. Kips could arrange him substantial credits, and expectations are not taxable—he wouldn't need to consult Monsieur Belmont. Albert, the bibs."

For the first time I noticed that there were no napkins by our places. Albert was fastening a bib round Mrs. Montgomery's neck. She gave a squeal of pleasure. *"Ecrevisses!* I love *écrevisses."*

"We haven't toasted the late lamented Monsieur Groseli," the Divisionnaire said, adjusting his bib. "I won't pretend that I ever liked that man."

"Hurry up then, while Albert fetches your din-

66

ner. To Monsieur Groseli. He only attended two of our dinners before dying of cancer, so I had no time to study his character. If I had known of the cancer I would never have invited him to join us. I expect my guests to entertain me for a much longer time. Ah, here is your dinner, so I can now begin my own."

Mrs. Montgomery gave a high shriek. "Why, this is porridge, cold porridge."

"Real Scotch porridge. You should appreciate it, with your Scotch name." Doctor Fischer gave himself a helping of caviar and poured himself out a glass of vodka.

"It will destroy all our appetite," Deane said.

"Don't be afraid of that. There is nothing to follow."

"This is going too far, Doctor Fischer," Mrs. Montgomery said. "Cold porridge. Why, it's totally inedible."

"Don't eat it then. Don't eat it, Mrs. Montgomery. By the rules you will only lose your little present. To tell you the truth I ordered porridge especially for Jones. I had thought of some partridges, but how could he have managed with one hand?"

To my astonishment I saw that the Divisionnaire and Richard Deane had begun to eat and Mr. Kips had at least picked up his spoon.

"If we could have a little sugar," Belmont said, "it might perhaps help."

"I understand that the Welsh—no, no, I remember, Jones, I mean the Scots—consider it a blasphemy to spoil their porridge with sugar. They even eat it, I am told, with salt. You may certainly have salt. Offer the gentlemen salt, Albert. Mrs. Montgomery has decided to go hungry."

"Oh no, I won't ruin your little joke, Doctor Fischer. Give me the salt. It can't make the porridge any worse than it is."

Within a minute or two to my wonder they were all eating in silence and with a grim intensity. Perhaps the porridge clogged their tongues. "You don't attempt yours, Jones?" Doctor Fischer asked me and he helped himself to a little more caviar.

"I'm not hungry enough."

"Nor rich enough," Doctor Fischer said. "For several years now I have been studying the greediness of the rich. 'To him that hath shall be given' —those cynical words of Christ they take very literally. 'Given' not 'earned,' you notice. The presents I hand out when the dinner is over they could easily afford to give themselves, but then they would have earned them if only by signing a check. The rich hate signing checks. Hence the success of credit cards. One card takes the place of a hundred checks. They'll do anything to get their presents for nothing. This is one of the hardest tests I've submitted them to yet, and look how quickly they are eating up their cold porridge, so that the time for the presents will arrive. You, I am afraid, will get nothing, if you don't eat."

"I have something of more value than your present waiting for me at home."

"Very gallantly put," Doctor Fischer said, "but don't be too confident. Women don't always wait. I doubt if a missing hand aids romance. Albert, Mr. Deane is ready for a second helping."

"Oh, no," Mrs. Montgomery said, "no, not second helpings."

"It's for the sake of Mr. Deane. I want to fatten him so that he can play Falstaff."

Deane gave him a furious look, but he accepted the second helping.

"I'm joking, of course. Deane could no more play Falstaff than Britt Ekland could play Cleopatra. Deane is not an actor: he is a sex object. Teenage girls worship him, Jones. How disappointed they would be if they could see him without his clothes. I have reason to believe that he suffers from premature ejaculation. Perhaps the porridge will slow you down, Deane, my poor fellow. Albert, another plate for Mr. Kips and I see Mrs. Montgomery is nearly ready. Hurry up, Divisionnaire, hurry up, Belmont. No presents before everyone has finished." I was reminded of a huntsman controlling his pack with a crack of the whip.

"Watch them, Jones. They are so anxious to be finished that they even forget to drink."

"I don't suppose Yvorne goes well with porridge."

"Have a good laugh at them, Jones. They won't take it amiss."

"I don't find them funny."

"Of course I agree that a party like this has a serious side, but all the same . . . Aren't you reminded a little of pigs eating out of a trough? You would almost think they enjoy it. Mr. Kips has spilled some porridge over his shirt. Clean him up, Albert."

"You revolt me, Doctor Fischer."

He turned his eyes toward me: they were like the polished chips of a pale blue stone. Some gray beads of caviar had lodged in his red mustache.

"Yes, I can understand how you feel. I sometimes feel that way myself, but my research must go on to its end. I won't give up now. Bravo, Divisionnaire. You are catching them up. You ply a good spoon, Deane, my boy, I wish your female admirers could see you at this moment, guzzling away."

"Why do you do it?" I asked.

"Why should I tell you? You are not one of us. You never will be. Don't count on your expectations from me."

"I don't."

"You have a poor man's pride, I see. After all, why shouldn't I tell you. You *are* a sort of son. I want to discover, Jones, if the greed of our rich friends has any limit. If there's a 'Thus far and no further.' If a day will come when they'll refuse to earn their presents. Their greed certainly isn't limited by pride. You can see that for yourself tonight. Mr. Kips, like Herr Krupp, would have sat down happily to eat with Hitler in expectation of favors, whatever was placed before him. The Divisionnaire has spilled porridge down his bib. Give him a clean one, Albert. I think that tonight will mark the end of one experiment. I am playing with another idea."

"You are a rich man yourself. Are there limits to *your* greed?"

"Perhaps I shall find out one day. But my greed is of a different kind to theirs. I'm not greedy for trinkets, Jones."

"Trinkets are harmless enough."

"I like to think that my greed is a little more like God's."

"Is God greedy?"

"Oh, don't think for a moment I believe in him any more than I believe in the devil, but I have always found theology an amusing intellectual game. Albert, Mrs. Montgomery has finished her porridge. You can take her plate. What was I saying?"

"That God is greedy."

"Well, the believers and the sentimentalists say that he is greedy for our love. I prefer to think that, judging from the world he is supposed to have made, he can only be greedy for our humiliation, and *that* greed how could he ever exhaust? It's bottomless. The world grows more and more miserable while he twists the endless screw, though he gives us presents—for a universal suicide would defeat his purpose—to alleviate the humiliations we suffer. A cancer of the rectum, a streaming cold, incontinence. For example, you are a poor man, so he gives you a small present, my daughter, to keep you satisfied a little longer."

"She's a very big alleviation," I said. "If it's God who gave her to me I'm grateful to him."

"And yet perhaps Mrs. Montgomery's necklace will last longer than your so-called love."

"Why should he wish to humiliate us?"

"Don't I wish to humiliate? And they say he

made us in his image. Perhaps he found he was a rather bad craftsman and he is disappointed in the result. One throws a faulty article into the dustbin. Do look at them and laugh, Jones. Have you no humor? Everyone has an empty plate but Mr. Kips, and how impatient they're all getting now. Why, Belmont is even finishing up his plate for him. I'm not sure it's quite in accordance with my rules, but I'll let it pass. Bear with me a moment longer, my friends, while I finish my caviar. You can untie their bibs, Albert."

10

"It was revolting," I said to Anna-Luise. "Your father must be mad."

"It would be a lot less revolting if he were," she said.

"You should have seen them scrambling for his presents—all except Mr. Kips—he had to go to the lavatory first to vomit. Cold porridge hadn't agreed with him. Compared with the Toads I must admit your father did keep a kind of dignity—a devilish dignity. They were all very angry with me because I hadn't played their game. I was like an unfriendly audience. I suppose I held a mirror up to them, so that they became conscious of how badly they were behaving. Mrs. Montgomery said that I should have been sent from the table as soon as I refused to eat the porridge. 'Any of you could have done the same,' your father said. 'Then what would you have done with all the presents?' she asked. 'Perhaps I would have doubled the stakes next time,' he said."

"Stakes? What did he mean?"

"I suppose he meant his bet on their greed against their humiliation."

"What *were* the prizes?"

"Mrs. Montgomery had a fine emerald set in platinum with a kind of diamond crown above it, as far as I could see."

"And the men?"

"Eighteen-karat-gold watches—quartz watches with computers and all the works. All except poor Richard Deane. He had that photograph of himself in a pigskin frame which I saw in the shop. 'You've only to sign it,' Doctor Fischer told him, 'to get any teenage girl you want.' He walked out in a rage and I followed him. He said he was never going back. He said, 'I don't need a photograph to get any girl I want,' and he got into his Mercedes sports car."

"He'll go back," Anna-Luise said. "That car was a present too. But you—you'll never go back, will you?"

"No."

"You promise?"

"I promise," I said.

But death, I was to argue later, annuls promises. A promise is made to a living person. A dead person is already not the same as the one who was alive. Even love changes its character. Love ceases to be happiness. Love becomes a sense of intolerable loss.

"And you didn't laugh at them?"

"There was nothing to laugh at."

"That must have disappointed him," she said.

No further invitation came: we were left in

peace, and what a peace it was that winter, deep as the early snow that year and almost as quiet. Snow fell as I worked (it came down that year before November was out), while I translated letters from Spain and Latin America, and the silence of the settled snow outside the great tinted glass building was like the silence which lay happily between us at home—it was as if she were there with me on the other side of the office table just as she would be there in the late evening across another table as we played a last gin rummy before bed.

11

At weekends in early December I would take her up to Les Diablerets for a few hours' skiing. I was too old to learn, but I sat in a café and read the *Journal de Genève*, glad to know that she was happy, looping like a swallow down the slopes in the below-zero whiteness. The hotels had begun opening to the snow as flowers to an early spring. They were going to have a wonderful Christmas season. I loved seeing her come in to the café to join me with the snow on her boots and the cold like candles lighting up her cheeks.

I said to her once, "I've never been so happy."

"Why do you say that?" she asked me. "You were married. You were happy with Mary."

"I was in love with her," I said. "But I never felt secure. She and I were the same age when we married, and I was afraid always that she would die the first and that's what she did. But I've got you for life—unless you leave me. And if you do, that will be my fault."

"What about me? You've got to go on living long enough so that we can go away—wherever it is one goes—together."

"I shall try."

"At the same hour?"

"At the same hour." I laughed and so did she. Death was not a serious subject to either of us. We were going to be together forever and a day—*le jour le plus long* we called it.

I suppose, though he had given us no sign of his continuing existence, that Doctor Fischer lingered all the same somewhere in the cave of my unconscious, for one night I had a vivid dream of him. He was dressed in a dark suit and he stood beside an open grave. I watched him from the other side of the hole and I called out to him in a tone of mockery, "Who are you burying, Doctor? Is it your Dentophil Bouquet that did it?" He raised his eyes and looked at me. He was weeping and I felt the deep reproach of his tears. I woke myself and Anna-Luise with a cry.

It is strange how one can be affected for a whole day by a dream. Doctor Fischer accompanied me to work: he filled the moments of inaction between one translation and another, and he was always the sad Doctor Fischer of my dream and not the arrogant Doctor Fischer whom I had seen presiding at his mad party, who mocked at his guests and drove them on to disclose the shameful depths of their greed.

That evening I said to Anna-Luise, "Do you think we've been too hard on your father?"

"What do you mean?"

"He must be a very lonely man in that great house by the lake."

"He has his friends," she said. "You've met them."

"They are not his friends."

"He's made them what they are."

Then I told her my dream. All she said was, "Perhaps it was my mother's grave."

"He was there?"

"Oh yes, he was there, but I didn't see any tears."

"The grave was open. In my dream there was no coffin, no minister, no mourners except himself— unless I was one."

"There were a lot of people at the grave," she said, "my mother was much loved. All the servants were there."

"Even Albert?"

"Albert didn't exist in those days. There was an old butler—I can't remember his name. He left after my mother died, and so did all the other servants. My father started life again with a lot of strange faces. Please don't let's talk about your dream anymore. It's like when you find an end of wool on a sweater. You pull at it and you begin to unravel the whole sweater."

She was right, it was as if my dream had started a whole process of unravelment. Perhaps we had been a little too happy. Perhaps we had escaped a little too far into a world where only the two of us existed. The next day was a Saturday and I didn't work on Saturdays. Anna-Luise wanted to find a cassette for her player (like her mother, she loved music), and we went to a shop in the old part of Vevey near the market. She wanted a new cassette of Mozart's Jupiter Symphony.

A small elderly man came to serve us from the back of the shop. (I don't know why I write "elderly," for I don't suppose he was much older than myself.) I was looking idly at an album of discs by a French television singer and he came to ask me if he could help. Perhaps what made him appear old to me was a kind of humble look, the look of a man who had reached the end of any expectation except of a small commission on the sales he made. I doubt if there was anybody else in that shop who would have heard of the Jupiter Symphony. Pop music formed the main part of the stock.

"Ah, the Forty-first Symphony," he said. "By the Vienna Symphony Orchestra. A very good rendering, but I don't think we have it in stock anymore. There is not much demand, I am afraid," he added with a timid smile, "for what I call real music. If you don't mind waiting I will go down and have a search in the stockroom." He looked over my shoulder to where Anna-Luise stood (her back was toward us) and he added, "While I'm there, isn't there perhaps any other symphony of Mozart . . . ?"

Anna-Luise must have heard him for she turned. "If you have the Coronation Mass," she said and stopped, for the man was staring at her with what to my eyes seemed almost an expression of terror. "The Coronation Mass," he repeated.

"Just let me see any symphonies you have of Mozart."

"Mozart," he echoed her again, but he made no movement to go.

"Yes, Mozart," she said impatiently, and she moved away to look at the cassettes on a revolving case. The man's eyes followed her.

"Pop music," she said, "nothing but pop music," revolving the case with her finger. I looked back at the assistant.

"I am sorry, monsieur," he said, "I will go at once and see." He moved slowly toward the door at the back of the shop, but in the doorway he turned and looked back, first at Anna-Luise and then at me. He said, "I promise . . . I will do my best . . ." It seemed to me like an appeal for help, as though he would be facing some terror down below.

I went toward him and asked him, "Are you all right?"

"Yes, yes. I have a little heart trouble, that is all."

"You shouldn't be working. I'll tell one of the other assistants . . ."

"No, no, sir. Please not. But if I may ask you something?"

"Of course."

"That lady you are with . . ."

"My wife?"

"Oh, your wife . . . she reminded me so much— I must seem absurd to you, impertinent— of a lady I once knew. Of course it was many years ago, and she would be old now . . . nearly as old as I am, and the young lady, your wife . . ."

And suddenly I realized who it was who stood there, supporting himself with one hand on the doorway, old and humble with no fight in him—

there never had been any fight in him. I said,
"She's Doctor Fischer's daughter, Doctor Fischer of
Geneva." He crumpled slowly at the knees as
though he were going down on them to pray, and
then his head struck the floor.

A girl who was showing a television set to a customer came running to help me. I was trying to
turn him over, but even the lightest body becomes
heavy when it's inert. Together we got him on his
back and she opened his collar. She said, "Oh, poor
Mr. Steiner."

"What's wrong?" Anna-Luise asked, leaving the
turntable of cassettes.

"A heart attack."

"Oh," she said, "the poor old man."

"Better ring for an ambulance," I told the girl.

Mr. Steiner opened his eyes. There were three
faces looking down at him, but he looked at only
one and he shook his head gently and smiled.
"Whatever happened, Anna?" he asked. In a few
minutes the ambulance came and we followed the
stretcher out of the shop.

In the car Anna-Luise said, "He spoke to me. He
knew my name."

"He said Anna, not Anna-Luise. He knew your
mother's name."

She said nothing, but she knew as well as I did
what that meant. At lunch she asked me, "What
was his name?"

"The girl called him Steiner."

"I never knew his name. My mother only called
him 'he.' "

At the end of lunch she said, "Will you go to the

81

hospital and see that he's all right? I can't go. It would only be another shock for him."

I found him in the hospital above Vevey, where a notice welcomes a new patient or an anxious visitor with a direction to the Centre Funéraire. Above, on the hill, the autoroute plays a constant concrete symphony. He shared his room with one old bearded man who lay on his back with wide-open eyes staring at the ceiling—I would have thought him dead if every now and then his eyes had not blinked without changing the direction of their stare at the white sky of plaster.

"It's kind of you to inquire," Mr. Steiner said, "you shouldn't have troubled. They are letting me out tomorrow on condition I take things easy."

"A holiday?"

"It's not necessary. I don't have to carry any weight. The girl looks after the television sets."

"It wasn't a weight that caused the trouble," I said. I looked at the old man. He hadn't stirred since I came in.

"You needn't trouble about him," Mr. Steiner said "He doesn't talk and he doesn't hear when you speak to him. I sometimes wonder what he's thinking. Of the long voyage ahead of him perhaps."

"I was afraid in the shop that you'd embarked on that voyage too."

"I'm not as lucky as that."

It was obvious that no conscious will in him had fought against death. He said, "She looks exactly like her mother did when she was that age."

"That gave you the shock."

"I thought at first it was my imagination. I used to look for likenesses in other women's faces for years after she died, and then I gave it up. But this morning you used *his* name. He's still alive, I suppose. I'd surely have read in the papers if he had died. Any millionaire gets an obituary in Switzerland. You must know him as you married his daughter."

"I've met him twice, that's all, and it's enough."

"You are not his friend?"

"No."

"He's a hard man. He doesn't even know me by sight, but he ruined me. He as good as killed her —though it was no fault of hers. I loved her, but she didn't love me. He had nothing to fear. It would never have happened again." He looked quickly at the old man and was reassured. "She loved music," he said, "Mozart in particular. I have a disc of the Jupiter at home. I'd like to give it to your wife. You could tell her I found it in the stockroom."

"We haven't a gramophone—only a cassette player."

"It was made before the days of cassettes," he said as a man might have referred to "before the days of motorcars."

I asked him, "What do you mean—it would never have happened again?"

"It was my fault—and Mozart's . . . and her loneliness. She wasn't responsible for her loneliness." He said with a touch of anger (perhaps, I thought, if he had been given enough time he might have learned how to fight), "Perhaps he knows now what loneliness is like."

"So you *were* lovers," I said. "I thought from what Anna-Luise told me it had never come to that."

"Not lovers," he said, "you mustn't call it that—not in the plural. She spoke to me next day, on the telephone, while he was at the office. We agreed it wasn't right—not right, I mean, for her to get mixed up with a lot of lies. There was no future in it for her. There wasn't much future for her anyway as it turned out."

"My wife says that she just willed herself to die."

"Yes. *My* will wasn't strong enough. It's strange, isn't it, she didn't love me and yet she had the will to die. I loved her and yet I hadn't enough will to die. I was able to go to the cemetery because he didn't know me by sight."

"So there was somebody there to cry for her—besides Anna-Luise and the servants."

"What do you mean? He cried. I saw him cry."

"Anna-Luise said he didn't."

"She's wrong. She was only a child. I don't suppose she noticed. It's not important anyway."

Who was right? I thought of Doctor Fischer at the party whipping on his hounds. I certainly couldn't imagine him crying, and what did it matter? I said, "You know you'd always be welcome. I mean my wife would be glad to see you. A drink one evening?"

"No," he said, "I'd rather not. I don't think I could bear it. You see, they look so much alike."

There was nothing more to be said after that. I never expected to see him again. I took it for granted that he had recovered this time, though his death would not have appeared in any paper. He was not a millionaire.

I repeated to Anna-Luise what he had told me. She said, "Poor Mother. But it was only a little lie. If it only happened once."

"I wonder how *he* found out." It was odd how seldom we named names. It was generally "he" or "she," but there was no confusion. Perhaps it was part of the telepathy that exists between lovers.

"She said that when he began to suspect—although there was nothing really to suspect—he put a thing on his telephone to record conversations. He told her so himself, so when *that* conversation took place he must have known. Anyway it wouldn't surprise me if she told him herself—and told him that it wouldn't happen again. Perhaps she lied to me because I was too young to understand. Holding hands and listening to Mozart together would have been almost the same as making love to me then—as it was to him—I mean my father."

"I wonder if he really wept at the funeral."

"I don't believe that—unless he wept to see his victim disappear. Or perhaps it was hay fever. She died in the hay fever season."

12

Christmas came down and covered the land in
snow up to the edge of the lake—one of the coldest
Christmases for many years, enjoyed by dogs and
children and skiers, but I didn't belong to any of
those categories. My office was very warmly heated,
but the garden outside looked blue through the
tinted glass and chilled me all the same. I felt much
too old for my job—to deal with chocolates all the
time, milk and plain, almond and hazel, seemed
work more suitable to a younger man or a girl.

I was surprised when one of my chiefs opened
the door of my office and let in Mr. Kips. It was as
if a cartoon had come to life; bent almost double,
Mr. Kips advanced with his hand held out, as
though it was in search of that lost dollar rather
than in welcome. My colleague said, in a tone of
respect I was unaccustomed to hear, "I believe you
have met Mr. Kips."

"Yes," I said, "at Doctor Fischer's."

"I didn't know that you knew Doctor Fischer."

"Mr. Jones is married to his daughter," Mr. Kips said.

I thought I saw a look of fear on the face of my chief. I had been up till now far beneath his notice and suddenly I represented a danger—for a son-in-law of Doctor Fischer's, might he not, with that influence behind him, find a place on the board?

Unwisely I couldn't help teasing him a little. "Dentophil Bouquet," I said, "tries to undo the damage we do in this building to the teeth." It was a very rash remark: it could be classed as disloyalty. Big business, like a secret service, demands loyalty from its employees more than honesty.

"Mr. Kips," my chief said, "is a friend of the managing director. He has a little problem of translation and the managing director would like you to help him."

"A letter I wish to send to Ankara," Mr. Kips said. "I want to attach a copy in Turkish to prevent misunderstanding."

"I will leave you together," my chief said, and when the door closed, Mr. Kips told me, "This is confidential, of course."

"I can see that."

Indeed I had seen it at the very first glance. There were references to Prague and Skoda, and Skoda to all the world means armaments. Switzerland is a land of strangely knotted business affiliations: a great deal of political as well as financial laundering goes on in that little harmless neutral state. The technical terms which had to be translated were all connected, I could see, with weapons. (For a short while I was in a world far removed from chocolates.) Apparently there was a firm called ICFC Inc. which was American and it was purchasing weapons, on behalf of a Turkish company, from Czechoslovakia. The final destination of the weapons—all small arms—was very unclear. A name which sounded as if it might be Palestinian or Iranian was somehow involved.

My Turkish is more rusty than my Spanish because I have less practice (we don't do much business with the land of Turkish Delight), and the letter took me quite a long while to translate. "I will get a fair copy typed," I told Mr. Kips.

"I would rather you did it yourself," Mr. Kips said.

"The secretary can't read Turkish."

"All the same . . ."

When I had finished typing, Mr. Kips said, "I realize you have done this in office time, but all the same perhaps a little present . . . ?"

"Quite unnecessary."

"Might I perhaps send a box of chocolates to your wife? Perhaps liqueur chocolates?"

"Oh, but you know, Mr. Kips, in this business we are never short of chocolates."

Mr. Kips, still bent nearly double so that his nose approached the desk, as though he were trying to find the elusive dollar by the smell, folded the letter and the original and tucked them away in his notecase. He said, "When we meet at Doctor Fischer's, you won't, of course, mention . . . This affair is most confidential."

"I don't think we'll ever meet there again."

"But why? At this season of the year, if the

88

weather is fine, never mind the snow, he usually gives the most magnificent party of all the year. Soon, I expect, we shall be getting our invitations."

"I've seen one party and that is enough for me."

"I must admit that the last party was perhaps a little crude. All the same it will go down in the memory of his friends as the Porridge Party. The Lobster Party was a good deal more entertaining. But then you never know what to expect with Doctor Fischer. There was the Quail Party which rather upset Madame Faverjon . . ." He sighed. "She was very attached to birds. You can't please everybody."

"But I suppose his presents always do, please I mean."

"He's very, very generous."

Mr. Kips began to make his bent-pin way to the door: it was as though the gray moquette were a map printed with the route which he had to follow. I called after him, "I met an old employee of yours. He works in a music shop. Called Steiner."

He said, "I don't remember the name," and continued without pausing along the route which had been traced for him on the moquette.

That night I told Anna-Luise of my encounter. "You can't get away from them," she said. "First poor Steiner and then Mr. Kips."

"Mr. Kips's business had nothing to do with your father. In fact he asked me not to mention our meeting if I saw your father."

"And you promised?"

"Of course. I don't intend ever to see him again."

"But now they've attached you to him by a secret,

haven't they? They don't intend to let you go. They
want you to be one of them. Otherwise they won't
feel safe."

"Safe?"

"Safe from being laughed at by someone on the
outside."

"Well, the fear of being laughed at doesn't seem
to deter them much."

"I know. Greed wins every time."

"I wonder what the Quail Party can have been
that so upset Madame Faverjon."

"Something beastly. You may be sure of that."

The snow continued to fall. It was going to be a
very white Christmas. There were blocks even on
the autoroute and Cointrin airport was closed for
twenty-four hours. It mattered nothing to us. It
was the first Christmas we had ever had together,
and we celebrated it like children with all the trim-
mings. Anna-Luise bought a tree and we laid our
presents for each other at its foot, gift-wrapped in
the shops with gay paper and ribbons. I felt more
like a father than a lover or a husband. That didn't
worry me—a father dies first.

On the eve of Christmas the snow stopped and
we went to the old abbey at Saint Maurice for midnight Mass and listened to that still more ancient
story of the Emperor Augustus' personal decree
and how all the world came to be taxed. We were
neither of us Roman Catholics, but this was the
universal feast of childhood. It seemed quite suitable to see Belmont there, listening carefully to the
decree of the Emperor, all by himself, as he had
been at our wedding. Perhaps the Holy Family

should have taken his advice and somehow evaded registration at Bethlehem.

He was waiting at the door when we came out, and we couldn't avoid him, dark suit, dark tie, dark hair, thin body and thin lips and an unconvincing smile. "Merry Christmas," he said, winking at us, and pressed an envelope into my hand like a tax demand. I could tell from the feel that it contained a card. "I don't trust the post," he said, "at Christmas." He waved his hand. "There's Mrs. Montgomery. I felt sure she would be here. She's very ecumenical."

Mrs. Montgomery wore a pale blue scarf over her pale blue hair, and I could see the new emerald in the hollow of her scrawny throat. "Ha ha, Monsieur Belmont and his cards as usual. And the young couple. A very happy Christmas to you all. I didn't see the General in church. I hope he's not ill. Ah! There he is." Yes, there the Divisionnaire certainly was, framed in the church doorway like a portrait of a Crusader, stiff as a ramrod in the back and in one rheumatic leg, with his conquistador nose and his fierce mustache—it was difficult to believe that he had never heard a shot fired in anger. He too was alone.

"And Mr. Deane," Mrs. Montgomery exclaimed, "surely he *must* be here. Why, he's always here if he's not filming somewhere abroad."

I could see we had made a very bad mistake. Midnight Mass at Saint Maurice was as social as a cocktail party. We would never have got away if at that moment Richard Deane had not appeared from the church, swollen and flushed with drink.

We just had time to notice that he had a pretty girl in tow before we escaped.

"Good God," Anna-Luise said, "a party of the Toads."

"We couldn't have known they would be there."

"I don't believe in all this Christmas business, only I *want* to believe—but the Toads . . . Why on earth do they go?"

"I suppose it's a Christmas habit like our tree. I went last year alone. For no reason. I expect they were all there, but I didn't know any of them in those days—in those days—it seems years ago. I didn't even know that you existed."

Lying happily in bed that night in the short interval between love and sleep, we could talk of the Toads humorously, as though they were a kind of comic chorus to our own story which was the only important one.

"Do you suppose that the Toads have souls?" I asked Anna-Luise.

"Doesn't everyone have a soul—I mean if you believe in souls?"

"That's the official doctrine, but mine is different. I think souls develop from an embryo just as we do. Our embryo is not a human being yet, it still has something of a fish about it, and the embryo soul isn't yet a soul. I doubt if small children have souls any more than dogs—perhaps that's why the Roman Catholic Church invented Limbo."

"Have you a soul?"

I think I may have one—shop-soiled but still there. If souls exist you certainly have one."

"Why?"

"You've suffered. For your mother. Small children don't suffer, or dogs, except for themselves."

"What about Mrs. Montgomery?"

"Souls don't dye their hair blue. Can you imagine her even asking herself if she has a soul?"

"And Monsieur Belmont?"

"He hasn't had the time to develop one. Countries change their tax laws every budget, closing loopholes, and he has to think up new ways to evade them. A soul requires a private life. Belmont has no time for a private life."

"And the Divisionnaire?"

"I'm not so sure about the Divisionnaire. He might just possibly have a soul. There's something unhappy about him."

"Is that always a sign?"

"I think it is."

"And Mr. Kips?"

"I'm not sure about him either. There's a sense of disappointment about Mr. Kips. He might be looking for something he has mislaid. Perhaps he's looking for his soul and not a dollar."

"Richard Deane?"

"No. Definitely not. No soul. I'm told he has copies of all his old films and he plays them over every night to himself. He has no time even to read the books of the films. He's satisfied with himself. If you have a soul you can't be satisfied."

There was a long silence between us. We should in the nature of things have fallen asleep, but each was aware that the other was awake, thinking the

93

same thought. My silly joke had turned serious. It was Anna-Luise who spoke the thought aloud.

"And my father?"

"He has a soul all right," I said, "but I think it may be a damned one."

13

I suppose there is a day in most lives when every trivial detail is held in the memory as though stamped in wax. Such a day proved for me to be the last day of the year—a Saturday. The night before we had decided to drive up in the morning to Les Paccots if the weather proved fine enough for Anna-Luise to ski. There had been a slight thaw on Friday, but Friday night it was freezing. We would go early before the slopes were crowded and have lunch together at the hotel there. I woke at half-past seven and rang the *météo* to find out the conditions. Everything was okay though caution was advised. I made some toast and boiled two eggs and gave her breakfast in bed. "Why two eggs?" she asked.

"Because you'll be half dead of hunger before lunch if you are going to be there when the ski lift opens." She put on a new sweater that I had given her for Christmas: heavy white wool with a wide red band round the shoulders: she looked wonderful in it. We started off at half-past eight. The road was not bad, but as the *météo* had announced there were icy patches, so I had to put on chains at Châtel St. Denis, and the ski lift was open before we arrived. We had a small argument at St. Denis. She wanted to make a long round from Corbetta and ski down the black *piste* from Le Pralet, but my anxiety persuaded her to come down the easier red *piste* to La Cierne.

I was secretly relieved that a number of people were already waiting to go up at Les Paccots. It seemed safer that way. I never fancied Anna-Luise skiing on an empty slope. It was too like bathing from an empty beach. One always fears there must be some good reason for the emptiness—perhaps an invisible pollution or a treacherous current.

"Oh dear," she said, "I wish I'd been the first. I love an empty *piste*."

"Safety in numbers," I said. "Remember what the road was like. Be careful."

"I'm always careful."

I waited until she was on the move and waved to her as she went up. I watched her until she was out of sight among the trees; I found it easy to pick her out because of the red band on the sweater. Then I went into the Hôtel Corbetta with the book I had brought with me. It was an anthology of prose and verse called *The Knapsack* made by Herbert Read and published in 1939, after the war broke out, in a small format so that it could be carried easily in a soldier's kit. I had never been a soldier, but I had grown attached to the book during the phony war. It whiled away many hours of waiting in the firemen's post for the blitz on London which never seemed to be coming, as the others played their compulsory round of darts wearing their gas masks. I have thrown away the book now, but some of the passages I read that day remain embedded in the wax, just as on that night in 1940 when I lost my hand. I remember clearly what I was reading when the siren sounded: it was, ironically, Keats's "Ode on a Grecian Urn":

> Heard melodies are sweet, but those unheard
>   Are sweeter

An unheard siren would certainly have been sweeter. I tried to reach the end of the ode, but I got no further than

> And, little town, thy streets for evermore
>   Will silent be . . .

before I had to move out of the relative safety of our burrow. By two o'clock in the morning the words returned to me like something I had picked in a *sortes Virgilianae* because there *was* a strange silence in the City streets—all the noise was overhead: the flap of flames, the hiss of water and the engines of the bombers saying, "Where are you? Where are you?" There was a kind of hush at the heart of the destruction before an unexploded bomb was somehow set off and tore the silence away at street level and left me without a hand.

I remember . . . but there is nothing about that day until the evening that I can forget . . . for instance I remember the slight altercation I had at the Hôtel Corbetta with the waiter because I wanted a window seat from which I could watch the road she would come along from the foot of the *piste* at La Cierne. The table had just served a previous occupant, and there was a used cup and saucer which I suppose the waiter didn't want to clear. He was a surly man with a foreign accent. I expect he was a temporary employee, for Swiss waiters are the most agreeable in the world, and I remember thinking that he wouldn't last long.

The time passed slowly without Anna-Luise. I grew tired of reading and I persuaded the waiter with the help of a two-franc piece to keep the table for me, and I added the promise that two of us would soon be taking a snack there when lunch-time came. A lot of cars were now arriving with skis on their roofs and quite a long queue had formed at the ski lift. One of the rescue team, who are always on duty at the hotel, was gossiping with a friend in the queue. "Last accident we had was Monday," he said. "Boy with a broken ankle. You always get them in the school holidays." I went to the little shop next to the hotel to see if I could find a French paper, but there was only the Lausanne daily which I had already scanned at breakfast. I bought a packet of Toblerone for us to eat as a dessert, for I knew that at the restaurant there would be only ice cream. Then I took a walk and watched the skiers on the *piste bleu,* the low debu-tante slopes, but Anna-Luise I knew would be out of sight far above, among the trees on the *piste rouge.* She was a very good skier: as I've already written, her mother had taken her out for the first time and had begun teaching her at the age of four. An icy wind was blowing and I went back to my table and read suitably enough Ezra Pound's "Seafarer":

Hung with hard ice-flakes, where hail-scur flew,
There I heard naught save the harsh sea
And ice-cold wave . . .

After that I opened the anthology at random and reached Chin Shengt'an's "33 Happy Moments." To me there always seems to be a horrible complacency about Oriental wisdom: "To cut with a sharp knife a bright green watermelon on a big scarlet plate of a summer afternoon. Ah, is not this happiness?" Oh yes, if one is a Chinese philosopher, well-to-do, highly esteemed, at ease with the world, above all safe, unlike the Christian philosopher who thrives on danger and doubt. Though I don't share the Christian belief I prefer Pascal. "Everyone knows that the sight of cats or rats, the crushing of a coal etc. may unhinge the reason." Anyway, I thought, I don't like watermelons. It amused me, however, to add a thirty-fourth happy moment just as complacent as Chin Shengt'an's. "To be sitting warm in a Swiss café, watching the white slopes outside, and knowing that soon the one you love will enter, with red cheeks and snow on her boots, wearing a warm sweater with a red band on it. Is not this happiness?"

Again I opened *The Knapsack* at random, but the *sortes Virgilianae* do not always work and I found myself faced with "The Last Days of Doctor Donne." I wondered why a soldier should be expected to carry that in his knapsack for comfort or reassurance and I tried again. Herbert Read had printed a passage from one of his own works called *Retreat from St. Quentin,* and I can still remember the gist, though not the exact words, I was reading when I laid the book down forever. "I thought this is the moment of death. But I felt no emotion. I recalled once reading how in battle when men are hit, they never feel the hurt till later." I looked up from the page. Something was happening by the ski lift. The man who had spoken about the boy with a broken ankle was helping another man to carry a stretcher to the ski lift. They had laid their skis on the stretcher. I stopped reading and for curiosity I went out. I had to wait for several cars to pass me before I got across the road and by the time I reached the ski lift the rescue team was already on the way up.

I asked someone in the queue what had happened. No one seemed very much interested. An Englishman said, "Some kid has fallen a cropper. It's always happening."

A woman said, "I think it's a practice for the *sauveteurs.* They telephone down from above and try to catch them off their guard."

"It's a very interesting exercise to watch," a second man said. "They have to ski down with the stretcher. It takes a lot of skill."

I went back to the hotel to get out of the cold—I could see just as well from the window, but most of the time I was watching the ski lift because almost any moment now Anna-Luise would be joining me. The surly waiter came and asked me whether I wanted to order: he was like a parking meter which indicated that my two francs of time had expired. I ordered yet another coffee. There was a stir among the group at the ski lift. I left my coffee behind and went across the road.

The Englishman whom I had heard making his guess that a child had been hurt was now telling everyone triumphantly. "It's a real accident. I was listening to them in the office. They were telephoning for an ambulance from Vevey."

Even then, like the soldier at St. Quentin, I didn't realize I had been hit, not even when the *sauveteurs* came along the road from La Cierne and laid the stretcher down with great care for the sake of the woman on it. She was wearing quite a different kind of sweater from the one I had given Anna-Luise—a red sweater.

"It's a woman," somebody said, "poor thing, she looks bad," and I felt the same momentary and automatic compassion as the speaker.

"Pretty serious," the triumphant man told us all. He was the nearest to the stretcher. "She's lost a lot of blood."

I thought from where I stood that she had white hair and then I realized that they had bandaged her head before bringing her down.

"Is she conscious?" a woman asked and the Englishman who knew all about it shook his head.

The small group diminished in number and curiosity as people took the ski lift up. The Englishman went and spoke to one of the *sauveteurs* in bad

French. "They think she's hurt her skull," he explained to all of us, like a television commentator translating. I had a direct view now. It was Anna-Luise. The sweater wasn't white anymore because of the blood.

I pushed the Englishman to one side. He grasped my arm and said, "Don't crowd her, man. She has to have air."

"She's my wife, you bloody fool."

"Really? I'm sorry. Don't take it rough, old man."

It was a matter of minutes, I suppose, though it seemed hours, before the ambulance arrived. I stood there watching her face and seeing no sign of life. I said, "Is she dead?" I must have seemed to them a bit indifferent.

"No," one of them assured me. "Just unconscious. A crack on the head."

"How did it happen?"

"Well, as far as we can make out, there was a boy who fell up there and sprained his ankle. He shouldn't have been up on the *piste rouge*—he should have been on the *piste bleu*. She came over a rise and she hadn't much time to avoid him. She would have been all right probably if she had swung right, but I suppose she had not much time to think. She swung left toward the trees—you know the *piste*—but the snow is hard and tricky after the thaw and the freeze and she went right into a tree at top speed. Don't worry. The ambulance will be here any moment now. They will fix her up at the hospital."

I said, "I'll be back. I've got to go and pay for my coffee."

The Englishman said, "I do apologize, old man. I never thought . . ."

"For God's sake go and piss off," I said.

The waiter was more surly than ever. He told me, "You reserved this table for lunch. I have had to turn away customers."

"There's one customer you'll never see again," I told him back, and I threw a fifty-centime piece on the table which fell on the floor. Then I waited by the door to see if he would pick it up. He did and I felt ashamed. But if it had been in my power I would have revenged myself for what had happened on all the world—like Doctor Fischer, I thought, just like Doctor Fischer. I heard the scream of the ambulance and I returned to the ski lift.

They gave me a seat beside her stretcher in the ambulance and I left our car behind. I told myself that I would pick it up one day when she was better, and all the time I watched her face, waiting for her to come out of this coma and recognize me. We won't go to that restaurant, I thought, when we return, we'll go to the best hotel in the canton and have caviar like Doctor Fischer. She won't be well enough to ski, and by that time probably the snow will have gone. We shall sit in the sun and I'll tell her how scared I was. I'll tell her about that damned Englishman—I told him to piss off and he pissed off—and she'll laugh. I looked again at her unchanging face. She might have been dead if her eyes had not been closed. Coma is like deep sleep. Don't wake up, I urged her in my mind, until they've given you drugs so that you won't feel pain.

The ambulance went crying down the hill to where the hospital lay and I saw the mortuary sign which I had seen dozens of times, but now I felt a dull anger about it and the stupidity of the authorities who had put it just there for someone like myself to read. It's got nothing to do with Anna-Luise and me, I thought, nothing at all.

The mortuary sign is all that I can complain about now. Everyone, when the ambulance arrived, was very efficient. Two doctors were waiting at the entrance for our arrival. The Swiss *are* very efficient. Think of the complex watches and precision instruments they make. I had the impression that Anna-Luise would be repaired as skillfully as they would repair a watch—a watch of more than ordinary value, a quartz watch, because she was Doctor Fischer's daughter. They learned that when I said I must telephone to him.

"To Doctor Fischer?"

"Yes, my wife's father."

I could tell from their manner that this watch carried no ordinary guarantee. She was already being wheeled away accompanied by the older doctor. I could see only the white bandages on her head which had given me the impression of old age.

I asked what I should tell her father.

"We shall know better after the X ray."

"You think it may be serious?"

The young doctor said with caution, "We have to consider any injuries to the skull as potentially serious."

"Shall I wait to telephone till after the X ray?"

"I think as Doctor Fischer has to come from Geneva you should perhaps tell him at once."

The implication of his advice didn't strike home to me until I was dialing. I could not at first recognize the voice of Albert when he answered.

I said, "I want to talk to Doctor Fischer."

"Who shall I say is speaking, sir?" This was his servile voice which I hadn't heard him use before.

"Tell him Mr. Jones—his son-in-law."

At once the voice became the familiar Albert voice. "Oh, Mr. Jones, is it? The doctor's busy."

"I don't care if he is. Put me through."

"He told me that he was on no account to be disturbed."

"This is urgent. Do as I tell you."

"It might cost me my job."

"It will certainly cost you your job if you don't put me through."

There was a long silence and then the voice returned—the voice of the insolent Albert and not the servile one. "Doctor Fischer says he's too busy to talk to you now. He can't be interrupted. He's preparing a party."

"I've got to speak to him."

"He says as how you are to put what you want in writing."

Before I had time to reply he had broken the connection.

The young doctor had slipped away while I was on the telephone. Now he came back. He said, "I'm afraid, Mr. Jones, there has to be an operation—

an immediate one. There are a lot of outpatients in the waiting room, but there's an empty room on the second floor where you could rest undisturbed. I'll come and see you immediately the operation is over."

When he opened the door of the empty room I recognized it, or I thought I did, as the room where Mr. Steiner had lain, but hospital rooms all look the same, like sleeping tablets. The window was open and the clang and clatter of the autoroute came in.

"Shall I close the window?" the young doctor asked. From his solicitude you would have thought I was the patient.

"No, no, don't bother. I'd rather have the air." But it was the noise I wanted. It is only when one is happy or undisturbed that one can bear silence.

"If there is anything you want, just ring," and he showed me the bell beside the bed. There was a thermos for ice water on the table and he checked to see whether it was full. "I'll be back soon," he said. "Try not to worry. We have had many worse cases."

There was an armchair for visitors and I sat in it and I wished that Mr. Steiner lay in the bed for me to talk to. I would even have welcomed the old man who couldn't speak or hear. Some words of Mr. Steiner came back to my mind. He had said of Anna-Luise's mother: "I used to look in other women's faces for years after she died and then I gave it up." The awful thing in that statement was "for years." Years, I thought, years . . . can one go on for years? Every few minutes I looked at my watch . . . two minutes gone, three minutes gone, once I was lucky and four and a half minutes had passed. I thought: Shall I be doing this until I die?

There was a knock on the door and the young doctor entered. He looked shy and embarrassed and a wild hope came to me: they had made a gaffe and the injury wasn't serious after all. He said, "I'm sorry. I'm afraid . . ." Then the words came out in a rush. "We hadn't much hope. She didn't suffer at all. She died under the anesthetic."

"Died?"

"Yes."

All I could find to say was, "Oh."

He asked, "Would you like to see her?"

"No."

"Shall we get you a taxi? Perhaps you wouldn't mind coming to the hospital tomorrow. To see the registrar. There are papers which have to be signed. Such a lot of paperwork always."

I said, "I'd rather finish with all that now. If it's the same to you."

14

I sent to Doctor Fischer the letter that he required. I wrote the dry facts of his daughter's death and I told him when and where she was to be buried. It was not the hay fever season so that I could expect no tears, but I thought he might possibly turn up. He didn't and there was no one to watch her being put into the ground, except the Anglican padre, our twice-weekly maid and myself. I had her buried in Saint Martin's cemetery in Gibraltan ground (in Switzerland the Anglican Church belongs to the diocese of Gibraltar) because she had to be put somewhere. I had no idea what religious faith Doctor Fischer would have claimed to hold or her mother—or in what church Anna-Luise had been baptized—we had not had sufficient time together to learn such unimportant details about one another. As an Englishman it seemed the easiest thing to bury her according to English rites, since nobody so far as I know has established agnostic cemeteries. Most Swiss in the Canton of Geneva are Protestant, and her mother had probably been buried in a Protestant cemetery, but Swiss Protestants believe seriously in their religion—the Anglican Church, with all its contradictory beliefs, seemed closer to our agnostic views. In the cemetery I half expected Monsieur Belmont to appear discreetly in the background as he had appeared at our wedding and again at the midnight Mass, but to my relief he wasn't there. So there was no one I had to speak to. I was alone, I could go back alone to our flat, it was the next best thing to being with her.

What to do when I was there I had decided beforehand. I had read many years ago in a detective story how it was possible to kill oneself by drinking a half pint of spirits in a single draft. As I remembered the story, one character challenged the other to drink what was apparently called a sconce (the writer was Oxford educated). I thought I would make certain by dissolving in the whisky twenty tablets of aspirin which was all I had. Then I made myself comfortable in the easy chair in which Anna-Luise used to sit and put the glass on the table beside me. I felt at peace and an odd sense of near-happiness moved in me. It seemed to me that I could spend hours, even days, like that, just watching the elixir of death in the glass. A few grains of the aspirin settled to the bottom of the glass and I stirred them with my finger until they dissolved. As long as the glass was there I felt safe from loneliness, even from grief. It was like the interim of relief between two periods of pain, and I could prolong this interim at will.

Then the telephone rang. I let it ring for a while,

but it disturbed the peace of the room like a neighbor's dog. I got up and went into the hall. As I lifted the receiver I looked back at the glass for reassurance, that promise of no long future. A woman's voice said, "Mr. Jones. It is Mr. Jones, isn't it?"

"Yes."

"This is Mrs. Montgomery." So the Toads had caught up with me after all.

"Are you still there, Mr. Jones?"

"Yes."

"I wanted to say . . . we've only just heard . . . how sorry we all are . . ."

"Thank you," I said and rang off, but before I could get back to my chair, the telephone sounded again. Reluctantly I returned.

"Yes?" I said. I wondered which one it would be this time, but it was still Mrs. Montgomery. How long it takes such women to say good-bye even on the telephone.

"Mr. Jones, you didn't give me time to speak. I have a message for you from Doctor Fischer. He wants to see you."

"He could have seen me if he had come to his daughter's funeral."

"Oh, but there were reasons . . . You mustn't blame him . . . He will explain to you . . . He wants you to go and see him tomorrow . . . Anytime in the afternoon . . ."

"Why can't he telephone himself?"

"He very much dislikes the telephone. He always uses Albert . . . or one of us if we are around."

"Then why doesn't he write?"

"Mr. Kips is away at the moment."

"Does Mr. Kips have to write his letters?"

"His business letters, yes."

"I have no business with Doctor Fischer."

"Something to do with a trust, I think. You will go, won't you?"

"Tell him," I said, "tell him . . . I will consider it."

I rang off. At least that would keep him guessing all the next afternoon, for I had no intention of going. All I wanted was to return to my chair and the half-pint glass of neat whisky: a little sediment of aspirin had formed again, and I stirred this with my finger, but the sense of happiness had gone. I wasn't alone anymore. Doctor Fischer seemed to permeate the room like smoke. There was one way to get rid of him and I drained the glass without drawing breath.

I had expected, judging from the detective story, that the heart would stop as suddenly as a clock, but I found I was still alive. I think now that the aspirin had been a mistake—two poisons can counteract each other. I should have trusted the detective novelist: such people are said to research carefully when it comes to medical details, and then, if I remember aright, the character who drank the sconce was already half drunk while I was dead sober. So it is that we often bungle our own deaths.

I wasn't, for a moment, even sleepy. I felt more than usually clear-headed as one does when a little drunk, and in my temporary clarity I thought: trust, trust, and the reason for Doctor Fischer's message suddenly came to me. Anna-Luise's money from her mother, I remembered, was held in some kind of a trust: she had received the income only. I had no idea to whom the capital would belong now, and I thought with hatred: He doesn't come to her funeral, but he's already thinking of the financial consequences. Perhaps he gets the money—the blood money. I remembered her white Christmas sweater stained with blood. He was as greedy as the Toads, I thought. He was a Toad himself—the King Toad of them all. Then suddenly, in the way that I had pictured death would come, I was struck down by sleep.

15

When I woke I thought that perhaps I had been asleep for an hour or two. My head was quite clear, but when I looked at my watch, the hands seemed to have mysteriously retreated. I looked out of the window, but the gray snow sky gave nothing away —it looked much as it had looked before I slept. A morning sky, an evening sky, take your pick. It was quite a while before I realized I had slept for more than eighteen hours, and then it was the chair I sat in and the empty glass which brought back to me the fact that Anna-Luise was dead. The glass was like an emptied revolver or a knife that had been broken uselessly on the bone of the chest. I had to begin to find another way to die.

Then I remembered the telephone call and Doctor Fischer's concern with the trust. I was a man sick with grief, and surely a sick man can be forgiven his sick thoughts. I wanted to humiliate Fischer, who had killed Anna-Luise's mother and ruined Steiner. I wanted to prick his pride. I wanted him to suffer as I was suffering. I would go and see him as he asked.

I borrowed a car from my garage and drove to Versoix. I realized my head was not so clear as I had believed. On the autoroute I nearly crashed into the back of a lorry turning into one of the exits, and it occurred to me that this could have been as good a death as the whisky—but then perhaps it would have failed me more completely. I might have been dragged out of the wreck a cripple unable afterward to compass my own destruction. I drove more carefully from then on, but my thoughts still wandered—to the distant spot of red which I had watched as it mounted on the ski lift toward the *piste rouge,* to the all-red sweater on the stretcher, and the bandages I had taken for the white hair of a stranger. I nearly missed the exit to Versoix.

The great white house stood above the lake like a pharaoh's tomb. It dwarfed my car, and the bell seemed to tinkle absurdly in the depths of the enormous grave. Albert opened the door. For some reason he was dressed in black. Had Doctor Fischer put his servant into mourning in his place? The black suit seemed to have changed his character for the better. He made no show of not recognizing me. He didn't sneer at me, but led the way promptly up the great marble staircase.

Doctor Fischer was not in mourning. He sat as he had done at our first meeting behind his desk (it was almost bare except for one large, obviously expensive Christmas cracker, shiny in scarlet and

gold) and he said as before, "Sit down, Jones."
Then there was a long silence. For once it seemed
that he was at a loss for words. I looked at the
cracker and he picked it up and put it down again
and the silence went on and on, so it was I who
eventually spoke. I accused him. "You didn't come
to your daughter's funeral."

He said, "She had too much of her mother in
her." He added, "She even looked like her, when
she grew up."

"That was what Mr. Steiner said."

"Steiner?"

"Steiner."

"So! Is that little man still living?"

"Yes. At least he was a few weeks ago."

"A bug is difficult to finish," he said. "They get
back into the woodwork where your fingernail
won't reach."

"Your daughter never did you any harm."

"She was like her mother. In character as much
as in face. She would have harmed you in the same
way given the time. I wonder what sort of Steiner
would have come out of the woodwork in your
case. Perhaps the garbage man. They like to humiliate."

"Is that what you brought me here to say?"

"Not all, but a little part of it, yes. I have been
thinking ever since the last party that I owe you
something, Jones, and I'm not in the habit of running up debts. You behaved better than the others."

"The Toads, you mean?"

115

"Toads?"

"That was your daughter's name for your friends."

"I have no friends," he said in the words of his servant Albert. He added, "These people are acquaintances. One can't avoid acquaintances. You mustn't think I dislike such people. I don't dislike them. One dislikes one's equals. I despise them."

"Like I despise you?"

"Oh, but you don't, Jones, you don't. You are not speaking accurately. You don't despise me. You hate me or think you do."

"I know I do."

He gave at that assurance the little smile which Anna-Luise had told me was dangerous. It was a smile of infinite indifference. It was the kind of smile which I could imagine a sculptor temerariously and heretically carving on the inexpressive armor-plated face of Buddha. "So Jones hates me," he said, "that is an honor indeed. You and I expect Steiner. And in a way for the same reason. My wife in one case, my daughter in the other."

"You never forgive, do you, even the dead?"

"Oh, forgiveness, Jones. That's a Christian term. Are you a Christian, Jones?"

"I don't know. I only know I've never despised anyone as I despise you."

"Again you are using the wrong term. Semantics are important, Jones. I tell you, you hate, you don't despise. To despise comes out of a great disappointment. Most people are not capable of a great disappointment, and I doubt if you are. Their expectations are too low for that. When one despises,

116

Jones, it's like a deep and incurable wound, the beginning of death. And one must revenge one's wound while there's still time. When the one who inflicted it is dead, one has to strike back at others. Perhaps, if I believed in God, I would want to take my revenge on him for having made me capable of disappointment. I wonder by the way—it's a philosophical question—how one would revenge oneself on God. I suppose Christians would say by hurting his son."

"Perhaps you are right, Fischer. Perhaps I shouldn't even hate you. I think you are mad."

"Oh, no, no, not mad," he said with that small unbearable smile of ineffable superiority. "You are not a man of great intelligence, Jones, or you wouldn't at your age be translating letters about chocolates for a living. But sometimes I have a desire to talk a little way above my companion's head. It comes on me suddenly even when I'm with one of my—what did my daughter call them?—Toads. It's amusing to watch how they react. None of them would dare to call me mad as you have done. They might lose an invitation to my next party."

"And lose a plate of porridge?"

"No, lose a present, Jones. They can't bear to lose a present. Mrs. Montgomery pretends to understand me. 'Oh, how I agree, Doctor Fischer,' she says. Deane gets angry—he can't bear anything which is beyond him. He says that even King Lear is a pack of nonsense because he knows that he is incapable of playing him, even on the screen. Belmont listens attentively and then changes the subject. Income taxes have taught him to be evasive.

The Divisionnaire . . . I have only broken out once with him when I couldn't bear the old man's stupidity anymore. All he did was give a gruff laugh and say, 'March to the sound of the guns.' Of course he has never heard a gun fired, only rifles on practice ranges. Kips is the best listener . . . I think he always hopes there may be a grain of sense in what I say which would be useful to him. Ah, Kips . . . he brings me back to the point of why I have brought you here. The Trust."

"What about the Trust?"

"You know—or perhaps you don't—that my wife left the income of her little capital to her daughter, but for life only. Afterward the capital goes to any child she may have had, but as she died childless it reverts to me. 'To show her forgiveness' the will impertinently states. As if I could care a cent for her forgiveness—forgiveness of what? If I were to accept the money it would really be as though I had accepted her forgiveness—the forgiveness of a woman who betrayed me with a clerk of Mr. Kips."

"Are you sure that she slept with him?"

"Slept with him? She may have dozed beside him over some caterwauling record. If you mean did she copulate with him, no, I am not sure of that. It's possible, but I'm not sure. It wouldn't have mattered to me very much if she had. An animal impulse. I could have put it out of mind, but she preferred his company to mine. A clerk of Mr. Kips earning a minimum wage."

"It's all a question of money, is it, Doctor Fischer? He wasn't rich enough to cuckold you."

"Money makes a difference certainly. Some people will even die for money, Jones. They don't die for love except in novels."

I thought I had tried to do just that, but I had failed, and was it for love I had tried or was it from the fear of an irremediable loneliness?

I had ceased to listen to him, and my attention only returned in time to catch the last of his words: "So the money is yours, Jones."

"What money?"

"The Trust money of course."

"I don't need it. We both of us managed on what I earned. On that alone."

"You surprise me. I thought you would at least have enjoyed while you could a little of her mother's money."

"No, we kept that untouched. For the child we meant to have." I added, "When the skiing stopped," and through the window I saw the continuous straight falling of the snow as though the world had ceased revolving and lay becalmed at the center of a blizzard.

Again I missed what he had been saying and caught only the final sentences. "It will be the last party I shall give. It will be the extreme test."

"You are giving another party?"

"The last party, and I want you to be there, Jones. I owe you something, as I said. You humiliated them at the Porridge Party more than I ever succeeded in doing till now. You didn't eat. You surrendered your present. You were an outsider and you showed them up. How they hated you. I enjoyed every moment of it."

"I saw them at Saint Maurice after the midnight Mass. They didn't seem to feel any resentment. Belmont even gave me a Christmas card."

"Of course. If they had exhibited their feelings it would have been a further humiliation. They have to explain you away. Do you know what the Divisionnaire said to me a week later (it was probably Mrs. Montgomery's idea): 'You were a bit hard on your son-in-law, not letting him have his present, poor fellow. It wasn't his fault that he had a bad attack of collywobbles that night. It could have happened to any one of us. I was a bit queasy myself as it happens, but I didn't want to spoil your joke.'"

"You won't get me to another party."

"This party is going to be a very serious party, Jones. No frivolity I promise. And it will be an excellent dinner, I promise that too."

"I'm not exactly in a *gourmand* mood."

"I tell you this party is the extreme test of their greed. You suggested to Mrs. Montgomery that I should give them checks, and checks they will have."

"She told me they'd never accept checks."

"We'll see, Jones, we'll see. They will be very, very substantial. I want you here as a witness of how far they'll go."

"Go?"

"For greed, Jones. The greed of the rich which you are never likely to know."

"You are rich yourself."

"Yes, but my greed—I told you before—is of a different order. I want . . . " He raised the Christmas cracker rather as the priest at midnight Mass had raised the Host, as though he intended to make a statement of grave importance to a disciple —"This is my body." He repeated: "I want . . ." and lowered the cracker again.

"What do you want, Doctor Fischer?"

"You aren't intelligent enough to understand if I told you."

That night for the second time I dreamed of Doctor Fischer. I thought I wouldn't sleep, but perhaps the long cold drive from Geneva helped sleep to come and perhaps in attacking Fischer I had been able to forget for half an hour how meaningless my life had become. I fell asleep as I had the day before, suddenly, in my chair, and I saw Doctor Fischer with his face painted like a clown's and his mustache trained upward like the Kaiser's as he juggled with eggs, never breaking one. He drew fresh ones from his elbow, from his arse, from the air—he created eggs, and at the end there must have been hundreds in the air. His hands moved around them like birds and then he clapped his hands and they fell to the ground and exploded and I woke. Next morning the invitation lay in my letter box: "Doctor Fischer invites you to the Final Party." It was to be held in a week's time.

I went to the office. People were surprised to see me, but what else was there to do? My attempt to die had failed. No doctor in the state I was in would prescribe me anything stronger than a tranquilizer. If I had the courage I could go up to the top floor of the building and throw myself out of the window—if any window there opened, which I doubted—but I hadn't got the courage. An "accident" with my car might involve others and anyway it was not certain to kill. I had no gun. I thought of all these things rather than of the letter I had to write to the Spanish confectioner who was still obsessed by the Basque taste in liqueur chocolates. After work I didn't kill myself but went to the first cinema on the way home and sat for an hour before a soft porn film. The movements of the naked bodies aroused no sexual feeling at all: they were like designs in a prehistoric cave—writings in the unknown script of people I knew nothing about. I thought when I left: One must, I suppose, eat, and I went to a café and had a cup of tea and a cake, and when I had finished I thought: Why did I eat? I needn't have eaten. That's a possible way to die, starvation, but I remembered the mayor of Cork who had survived for more than fifty days, wasn't it? I asked the waitress for a piece of paper and wrote on it: "Alfred Jones accepts Doctor Fischer's invitation," and I put it in my pocket to guard against a change of mind. Next day I posted it almost without thinking.

Why had I accepted the invitation? I don't know myself. Perhaps I would have accepted any engagement which would give me an hour or two's escape from thought—thought which consisted mainly of wondering how I could die without too much pain for myself or too much unpleasantness for others. There was drowning: Lake Léman was only a short walk down the street—the ice-cold water would soon conquer any instinctive desire I might have to swim. But I hadn't the courage—death by drowning had been a phobia of mine since childhood ever since I had been pushed into the deep end of a *piscine* by a young Secretary of Embassy. Besides, my body might pollute the perch. Gas came to mind, but my flat was all electric. There were the fumes of my car, of course—I'd kept that idea in reserve, for after all starvation might perhaps be the proper answer, a clean and discreet and private way out: I was older, and less robust probably, than the mayor of Cork. I would fix a date for beginning —the day after Doctor Fischer's feast.

16

Ironically I was delayed on the autoroute by an accident: a private car had smashed itself against a lorry on a frozen patch of the road. The police were there and an ambulance, and something was being removed from the wreck of the car with the help of an acetylene burner which flamed so brightly in the dark that it made the night twice as black when I passed. Albert was already standing by the open door when I arrived. His manner had certainly improved (perhaps I had been accepted as one of the Toads), for he came down the steps to greet me and opened the door of the car and for the first time he allowed himself to remember my name. "Good evening, Mr. Jones, Doctor Fischer suggests that you keep on your coat. Dinner is being served on the lawn."

"On the lawn?" I exclaimed. It was a clear night: the stars were as brilliant as chips of ice, and the temperature was below zero.

"I think you will find it warm enough, sir."

He led me through the lounge in which I had first met Mrs. Montgomery and then through another room, where the walls were lined with books in expensive calf bindings—they had probably been bought in sets ("The library, sir."). It would have been much cheaper, I thought, to have used false backs, for the room had an unused air. French windows opened on to the great lawn which sloped down to the invisible lake and for a moment I could see nothing at all but a blaze of light. Four enormous bonfires crackled away across the snow, and lights were hanging from the branches of every tree.

"Isn't it wonderful and crazy and beautiful?" Mrs. Montgomery cried, as she advanced from the edge of the dark to meet me with the assured air of a hostess addressing an intimidated guest. "Why, it's a real fairyland. I don't believe you'll even need your coat, Mr. Jones. We are all of us so glad to see you back among us. We've quite missed you." "We" and "us"—I could see them now undazzled by the bonfires; the Toads were all there, standing around a table prepared in the center of the fires; it glittered with crystal glasses which reflected the to and fro of the flames. The atmosphere was very different from what I remembered of the Porridge Party.

"Such a shame that this is the very last party," Mrs. Montgomery said, "but you'll see how he's giving us a really great farewell. I helped him with the menu myself. No porridge!"

Albert was suddenly beside me, holding a tray of glasses, whisky, dry martinis and Alexanders. "I am an Alexander girl," Mrs. Montgomery said. "This is my third. How absurd it is when people tell you that cocktails spoil the palate. What I always say is, it's just not-feeling-hungry that spoils the palate."

Richard Deane in his turn came out of the shadows carrying a gold-embossed menu. I could see he was already well plastered, and there beyond him, between two bonfires, was Mr. Kips, who actually seemed to be laughing: it was difficult to be quite sure because of his stoop, which hid his mouth, but his shoulders were certainly shaking. "This is better than porridge," Deane said, "what a pity that it's the last party. Do you think the old fellow's running out of cash?"

"No, no," Mrs. Montgomery said. "He always told us that one day there would be the last and the best and the most exciting party of all. Anyway I don't think he has the heart to go on any longer. After what's happened. His poor daughter . . ."

"Has he a heart?" I asked.

"Ah, you don't know him as all of us do. His generosity . . ." With the automatic reflex of a Pavlov dog she touched the emerald hung around her throat.

"Drink up and seat yourselves."

It was Doctor Fischer's voice which brought us to heel from a dark corner of the garden. I hadn't seen until then where he was standing. He was stooped over a barrel some twenty yards away, and I could see his hands moving within it as though he were washing them.

"Just look at the dear man," Mrs. Montgomery

said. "He takes such an interest in every small detail."

"What's he doing?"

"He's hiding the crackers in the bran tub."

"Why not have them on the table?"

"He doesn't want people crackling them all through dinner to find out what's inside. It was I who told him about the bran tub. Just fancy, he had never heard of such a thing before. I don't think he can have had a very happy childhood, do you? But he took to the idea at once. You see, he's put the presents in the crackers and the crackers in the bran tub and we'll all have to draw them out at random with our eyes shut."

"Suppose you get a gold cigar cutter?"

"Impossible. These presents have been chosen to suit everyone equally."

"What is there in the world which can possibly suit everyone?"

"Just wait and see. He'll tell us. Trust him. At bottom, you know, he's a very sensitive sort of person."

We sat down at the table. I found myself seated this time between Mrs. Montgomery and Richard Deane, and opposite me were Belmont and Mr. Kips. The Divisionnaire was at the end of the table facing our host. The array of glasses was impressive and the menu informed me that there would be a 1971 Meursault, a 1969 Mouton Rothschild, and I can't remember the date of the Cockburn port. At least, I thought, I can drink myself stupid without the help of aspirin. The bottle of Finnish vodka, served with the caviar (this time the caviar was handed to all of us), was enclosed in a solid block of ice in which the petals of hothouse flowers had been frozen. I took off my overcoat and hung it on the back of my chair to guard me from the heat of the bonfire behind. Two gardeners like sentries moved to and fro, their steps unheard on the deep white carpet of the snow, feeding the flames with logs of wood. It was a curiously unnatural scene—so much heat and so much snow, and the snow beneath our chairs was already beginning to melt from the warmth of the bonfires. Soon, I thought, we shall be sitting with our feet in slush.

The caviar in a great bowl was served to us twice, and everyone but myself and Doctor Fischer took a second helping. "It's so healthy," Mrs. Montgomery explained. "Full of vitamin C."

"I can drink Finnish vodka with a good conscience," Belmont told us, accepting a third glass.

"They fought a remarkable campaign in the winter of 1939," the Divisionnaire said. "If the French had done as well in '40 . . ."

Richard Deane asked me, "Did you by any chance see me in *The Beaches of Dunkirk?*"

"No. I wasn't at Dunkirk."

"It's the film I meant."

"No. I'm afraid I never saw it. Why?"

"I just wondered. I think it was quite the best film I ever made."

With the Mouton Rothschild there was a *rôti de boeuf*. It had been cooked in a very light pastry which preserved all the juice of the meat. A magnificent dish, of course, but for a moment the sight of the red blood sickened me—I was back at the foot of the ski lift. "Albert," Doctor Fischer said, "you must cut up Mr. Jones's meat for him. He has a deformed hand."

"Poor Mr. Jones," Mrs. Montgomery said. "Let me do it. Do you like the pieces cut small?"

"Pity, always pity," the Doctor said. "You ought to rewrite the Bible. 'Pity your neighbor as you pity yourself.' Women have such an exaggerated sense of pity. My daughter took after her mother in that. Perhaps she married you out of pity, Jones. I'm sure Mrs. Montgomery would marry you if you asked her. But pity wears off quickly, when the pitied one is out of sight."

"What emotion doesn't wear off?" Deane asked.

"Love," Mrs. Montgomery replied promptly.

"I've never been able to sleep with the same woman for more than three months," Deane said. "It becomes a chore."

"Then that isn't real love."

"How long were you married, Mrs. Montgomery?"

"Twenty years."

"I must explain to you, Deane," Doctor Fischer said, "that Mr. Montgomery was a very rich man. A big bank balance helps real love to last longer. But you aren't eating, Jones. Don't you find the beef tender enough, or perhaps Mrs. Montgomery hasn't cut it up in small enough pieces?"

"The meat is excellent, but I have no appetite."
I helped myself to another glass of Mouton Roths-

child; it wasn't for the flavor of the wine that I drank it, for my palate seemed dead, it was for the distant promise of a sort of oblivion.

"In the normal course, Jones," Doctor Fischer said, "you would have lost your prize by not eating, but at this last party of ours no one will forfeit a prize except by his own express wish."

"Who could possibly refuse one of *your* presents, Doctor Fischer?" Mrs. Montgomery asked.

"That is what in a few minutes I shall be very interested to discover."

"You know it could never happen, you generous man."

"Never is a big word. I'm not so sure that tonight . . . Albert, you are neglecting the glasses. Mr. Deane's is almost empty, and so is Monsieur Belmont's."

It was not until we had begun to drink the port (at the end of the meal, in the English manner, served with Stilton) that he explained his meaning. As usual it was Mrs. Montgomery who set him off.

"My fingers are itching," she said, "to get at that bran pie."

"Just a lot of crackers," Doctor Fischer said. "Mr. Kips, you really mustn't fall asleep until you pull your cracker. You are blocking the port, Deane. No. Not that way. Where were you educated? Clockwise."

"Just crackers," Mrs. Montgomery said. "You silly man. We know better. It's what's in the crackers that counts."

"Six crackers," Doctor Fischer said, "and five contain the same pieces of paper."

"Pieces of paper?" Belmont exclaimed and Mr. Kips tried to swivel his head in Doctor Fischer's direction.

"Mottoes," Mrs. Montgomery explained. "All good crackers contain mottoes."

"But what else?" Belmont demanded.

"There are no mottoes," Doctor Fischer said. "These pieces of paper are printed with a certain name and address—Crédit Suisse, Berne."

"Surely not checks?" Mr. Kips asked.

"Checks, Mr. Kips, and each one made out for the same sum, so that nobody need feel jealous."

"I don't much like the idea of checks between friends," Belmont said. "Oh, I know you mean to be kind, Doctor Fischer, and we've all appreciated the little presents you have often given us at the end of a party, but checks—it's not . . . well . . . not very dignified, is it, apart from any fiscal problems?"

"I'm paying you all off—that's what it amounts to."

"We are not your employees, damn it," Richard Deane said.

"Are you so sure of that? Haven't you all played your parts for my amusement and your profit? Deane, you for one must have felt quite at home taking my orders. I've been just another director, who lends you a talent you don't possess yourself."

"I don't have to accept your bloody check."

"You don't have to, Deane, but you will. Why, you'd play Mr. Darling in *Peter Pan* shut up in a dog kennel if the check was large enough."

"We've had an excellent dinner," Belmont said,

"which we'll always remember with appreciation. We mustn't get overexcited. I can understand Deane's point, but I do think he exaggerates."

"Of course you are quite at liberty to refuse my little farewell presents if you wish. I will tell Albert to take away the bran tub. Albert, did you hear me? Take the bran tub to the kitchen—no, wait one moment. Before you decide, I think you ought to know what is written on those scraps of paper. Two million francs on each."

"Two million!" Belmont exclaimed.

"The name is left blank on all the checks. You can fill in what name you wish. Perhaps Mr. Kips would like to donate his check to some medical research on curing curvature of the spine. Mrs. Montgomery may even want to buy a lover. Deane can partly finance a film. He is in danger of becoming what I believe in his world is called unbankable."

"It doesn't seem quite proper," Mrs. Montgomery said. "It sort of suggests that you think us mercenary friends."

"Didn't your emerald suggest that?"

"Jewels from a man one loves are quite different. You don't realize, Doctor Fischer, how much we love you. Platonic perhaps, but is platonic less real than, well . . . you know what I mean."

"Of course I'm aware that not one of you needs two million francs to spend on yourselves. You are all rich enough to give the money away—though I wonder if any of you will."

"It does make a certain difference," Belmont said, "that our names are not on the checks."

"Taxwise," Doctor Fischer said, "I felt sure it would be more convenient. But you know better about such things than I do."

"I was not thinking of that. I was thinking of human dignity."

"Ah, yes, I understand you really mean that it's more difficult to feel insulted by a check for two million francs than one for two thousand."

"I would have phrased it differently," Belmont said.

For the first time the Divisionnaire spoke. He said, "I am not a financier like Mr. Kips or Monsieur Belmont. I am only a simple soldier, but I cannot see the difference between accepting caviar and accepting a check."

"Bravo, General," Mrs. Montgomery said. "It was just what I was going to say myself."

Mr. Kips said, "I made no objection. I only asked a question."

"I too," Belmont said. "As our names are not on the checks . . . I was only trying to be wise for all of us—especially for Mr. Deane, who is English. It's my duty as his tax consultant."

"You advise me to accept?" Deane asked.

"Under the circumstances, yes."

"You can leave the bran tub where it is, Albert," said Doctor Fischer.

"There is something unexplained," Mr. Kips said. "You have mentioned six crackers and five pieces of paper. Is this because Mr. Jones is not taking part?"

"Mr. Jones will have the same chance as any of you. In turn you will go to the bran tub and fish for your cracker—you will pull it while you stand by the bran tub and then return to the table. That is to say if you return at all."

"What do you mean—if?" Deane asked.

"I suggest, before I answer your question, that you all take another glass of port. No, no, please, Deane. I told you before—not anticlockwise."

"You are making us quite tiddly," Mrs. Montgomery said.

Deane said, "You haven't answered Mr. Kips's question. Why only five pieces of paper?"

"I drink to the health of all of you," Doctor Fischer said, raising his glass. "Even if you refuse to draw your cracker, you will deserve your dinner, for you are helping me in my last piece of research."

"What research?"

"Into the greed of the rich."

"I don't understand."

"Dear Doctor Fischer. It's one of his little jokes," Mrs. Montgomery said. "Drink up, Mr. Deane."

They all drank. I could tell they were more than a little intoxicated—it was only I who seemed hopelessly condemned to the sadness of sobriety however much I drank. I left my glass empty. I was determined to drink no more before I was at home alone and I could drink myself to death if I chose.

"Jones doesn't drink our toast. Never mind. Tonight all our rules are relaxed. I have for a long time wanted to test the strength of your greed. You have submitted to a great deal of humiliation and you have accepted it for the sake of the prize which followed. Our Porridge Party was merely the final

134

test. Your greed was greater than any humiliation that I had the imagination to invent."

"There was no humiliation, you dear man. It was just your wonderful sense of humor. We enjoyed it all as much as you did."

"Now I want to see whether your greed can even overcome your fear—and so I have organized what I would call . . . a Bomb Party."

"What the hell do you mean, Bomb Party?" Deane's drinks had made him aggressive.

"The sixth cracker contains a small charge, lethal probably, which will be set off by one of you when he pulls the cracker. That is why the bran tub is set at a good distance from our table, and that is why the crackers are well buried and the bran tub covered by a lid in case of a spark landing there from one of the bonfires. I may add that it would be useless—indeed perhaps dangerous—for you to crinkle your crackers. They all hold the same type of metal container, but in only one container is there what I call the bomb. In the others are the checks."

"He's joking," Mrs. Montgomery told us.

"Perhaps I am. You will know by the end of the party whether I am or not. Isn't the gamble worthwhile? Death is by no means certain, even if you choose the dangerous cracker, and I give you my word of honor that the checks anyway are really there. For two million francs."

"But if someone was killed," Belmont said, winking rapidly, "why, it would be murder."

"Oh, not murder. I have you all as witnesses. A form of Russian roulette. Not even suicide. I am sure Mr. Kips will agree with me. Anyone who doesn't wish to play should leave the table at once."

"I am certainly not going to play," said Mr. Kips. He looked around for support but he found none. "I refuse to be a witness. There will be a great scandal, Doctor Fischer. It's the least you can expect."

He rose from the table and, as he paced his back-bent way between the bonfires toward the house, I was again reminded of a little black seven. It seemed odd that a man so handicapped should be the first to refuse the risk of death.

"There are five chances to one in your favor," Doctor Fischer told him as he passed.

"I have never gambled for money," Mr. Kips said. "I consider it highly immoral."

In a strange way his words seemed to lighten the atmosphere. The Divisionnaire said, "I don't see any immorality in gambling. I have passed many a happy week at Monte Carlo. I once won three times consecutively on nineteen."

"Sometimes I have been across the lake to the casino in Evian," Belmont said. "Never high stakes. But I am by no means a puritan in these matters." It was as if they had quite forgotten the bomb. Perhaps it was only I and Mr. Kips who believed that Doctor Fischer had spoken the truth.

"Mr. Kips took you too seriously," Mrs. Montgomery said. "He has no sense of humor."

"What will happen to Mr. Kips's check," Belmont asked, "when his cracker remains unpicked?"

"I shall divide it between you. Unless of course it contains the charge. You would hardly want me to divide that."

"Another four hundred thousand francs each," Belmont calculated quickly.

"No. More than that. One of you will probably not have survived."

"Survived!" Deane exclaimed. Perhaps he had been too drunk to take in the story of the explosive cracker.

"Of course," Doctor Fischer said, "all may very well end on a happy note. The sixth cracker may be the one that contains the bomb."

"Are you seriously saying there's a bloody bomb in one of the crackers?"

"Two million five hundred thousand francs," Mrs. Montgomery murmured—she had obviously corrected Belmont's figures and she was certainly dreaming of what Doctor Fischer had described as a happy ending.

"You, Deane, I am sure, will not refuse the little gamble. I remember how in *The Beaches of Dunkirk* you bravely volunteered for a suicidal action. You were splendid—at least you were splendidly directed. You very nearly won an Oscar, didn't you? 'I will go, sir, if I may go alone.' That was the great line I shall always remember. Who wrote it?"

"I wrote it myself. Not the scriptwriter or the director. It came to me suddenly like that, on the set."

"Congratulations, my boy. Now, here's your big chance to go to the bran tub alone."

I never expected Deane to go. He stood up and drained his port, and I thought he was going to follow Mr. Kips. But perhaps in drink he really believed he was back on a film set and an imaginary Dunkirk. He touched the side of his head as though he were adjusting a nonexistent beret, but while he was thinking himself back into his old role Mrs. Montgomery acted. She left the table and ran across the snow to the bran tub, crying, "Ladies first," knocked off the lid and plunged her hand into the bran. Perhaps she had calculated that the odds would never be as favorable again.

Belmont had probably been thinking along the same lines, for he protested, "We should have drawn for turns."

Mrs. Montgomery found her cracker and pulled. There was a small pop and a little metal cylinder fell onto the snow. She poked out a roll of paper and gave a scream of excitement.

"What's wrong?" Doctor Fischer asked.

"Nothing's wrong, you dear man. Everything's splendidly right. Crédit Suisse, Berne. Two million francs." She ran back to the table. "Give me a pen, somebody. I want to fill in my name. It might get lost."

"I would advise you not to fill in your name until we have considered things very carefully," Belmont said, but he was speaking to a deaf woman. Richard Deane stood stiffly to attention. At any moment, I thought, he will salute his colonel. He must in his mind have been listening to the last orders he had been given, and Belmont had the time he needed to reach the bran tub before him. He hesitated a little before pulling his cracker out: the same small cylinder: the same paper, and he gave a little smile of self-satisfaction and his eye winked. He had calculated the odds—he had been right to bet. He was a man who knew all about money.

Deane said, "I will go, sir, if I may go alone."

All the same, he didn't go. Perhaps the director at that moment had ordered "Cut."

"What about you, Jones?" Doctor Fischer said. "The odds are narrowing."

"I prefer to watch your damned experiment to the end. Greed is winning, isn't it?"

"If you watch you must eventually play—or leave like Mr. Kips."

"Oh, I'll play, I promise you that. I'll bet on the last cracker. That gives better odds to the Divisionnaire."

"You're a stupid and boring man," Doctor Fischer said, "there's no credit in choosing death if you want to die. What in God's name is Deane doing?"

"I think he's improvising."

Deane was still by the table, pouring out another glass of port, but no one this time had taken advantage of the delay, for only myself and the Divisionnaire were left.

"Thank you, sir," Deane said. "It's a kind thought. Dutch courage never did anyone any harm. . . . Quite unnecessary in your case, Captain, I know. . . . Thank you, sir, but the more unnecessary it is, the better the flavor. . . . If you come back safely we'll split another bottle. . . . Cockburn's, like this, I hope, sir."

I wondered if he would spin the dialogue out till dawn, but at the last sentence he put down his glass, saluted smartly and marched to the bran tub, fumbled for a cracker, pulled it, and fell on the ground beside the cylinder and the check.

"Dead drunk," Doctor Fischer said and told the gardeners to carry him into the house.

The Divisionnaire looked at me from the end of the table. He asked, "Why did you stay, Mr. Jones?"

"I have nothing better to do with my time, General."

"Don't call me that. I'm not a General. I am a Divisionnaire."

"Why have *you* stayed, Divisionnaire?"

"It's too late to turn tail now. I haven't the courage. I should have gone to the tub first, when the odds were better. What was that man Deane saying?"

"I think he was acting a young captain who volunteers for a desperate mission."

"I am a Divisionnaire, and Divisionnaires don't go on desperate missions. Besides, there *are* no desperate missions in Switzerland. Unless this is the exception. Will you go first, Mr. Jones?"

"What do you think of convertible bonds?" I heard Mrs. Montgomery ask Belmont.

"You have too many already," Belmont said, "and I think it will be a long time before the dollar recovers."

"I suggest you go first, Divisionnaire. I'm not in need of money and it gives you the better odds. I'm after something else."

140

"When I was a boy," the Divisionnaire said, "I used to play at Russian roulette with a cap pistol. It was very exciting." He made no move to go.

I could hear Belmont saying to Mrs. Montgomery, "I am thinking myself of investing in something German. For example Badenwerk of Karlsruhe pay eight and five-eighths percent—but then there's always the danger of Russia, isn't there? A rather unpredictable future."

As the Divisionnaire seemed unwilling to move, I did. I wanted to bring the party to an end.

I had to sort through a lot of bran before I found a cracker. Unlike the boy with a cap pistol, I felt no excitement—only a quiet sense when I touched the cracker that I was closer to Anna-Luise than I had been since I waited in the hospital room and the young doctor came to tell me she was dead. I held the cracker as though I were holding her hand, while I listened to the conversation at the table.

Belmont said to Mrs. Montgomery, "I have rather more confidence in the Japanese. Mitsubishi pay only six and three-quarters, but it's not worth taking unnecessary risks with two million."

I found the Divisionnaire was at my side.

"I think we ought to go now," Mrs. Montgomery said. "I am afraid something may be going to happen, though of course in my heart of hearts I am sure Doctor Fischer has only been having a little joke with us."

"If you would like to send your car home with the chauffeur, I will drive you back and we can discuss your investments on the way."

"Surely you will wait till the end of the party?" Doctor Fischer asked. "It won't be long delayed now."

"Oh, it's been a wonderful last party, but it's getting too late for little me." She fluttered her hands at us. "Good night, General. Good night, Mr. Jones. Wherever is Mr. Deane?"

"On the kitchen floor, I suspect. I hope Albert doesn't take his check. He would certainly give notice, and I should lose a good manservant."

The Divisionnaire whispered to me, "Of course, we might just walk away and leave him? If you would come with me. I don't want to go alone."

"In my case I have nowhere to walk to."

In spite of the whisper, Doctor Fischer had heard him. "You knew the rules of the game from the start, Divisionnaire. You could have left with Mr. Kips before the game started. Now because the odds are not so good, you begin to be afraid. Think of your honor as a soldier as well as the prize. There are still two million francs in that tub."

But the Divisionnaire did not move. He looked at me with the same appeal. When one is afraid, one needs company. Doctor Fischer went mercilessly on: "If you act quickly, the odds are two to one in your favor."

The Divisionnaire shut his eyes and found his cracker at the first dip, but he still stood irresolute beside the tub.

"Come back to the table, Divisionnaire, if you are afraid to pull, and give Mr. Jones his chance."

The Divisionnaire looked at me with the sad expressive eyes of a spaniel who tries to hypnotize his master into uttering the magic word "walk." I said, "I was the first to take out a cracker. I think you should allow me to pull mine first."

"Of course. Of course," he said. "It is your right."

I watched him until he had returned to the safe distance of the table, carrying his cracker with him. With my left hand gone it was not easy for me to pull a cracker. While I hesitated I was aware of the Divisionnaire watching me, watching as I thought, with hope. Perhaps he was praying—after all, I had seen him at the midnight Mass, he might well be a believer, perhaps he was saying to God, "Please, gentle Jesus, blow him up." I would probably have made much the same prayer—"Let this be the end"—if I had believed, and didn't I have at least a half-belief, or why was it that as long as I held the cracker in my hand I felt the closeness of Anna-Luise? Anna-Luise was dead. She could only continue to exist somewhere if God existed. I put one end of the protruding paper tape between my teeth and I pulled with the other end. There was a feeble crack, and I felt as though Anna-Luise had withdrawn her hand from mine and walked away, between the bonfires, down toward the lake to die a second time.

"Now, Divisionnaire," Doctor Fischer said, "the odds are even." I had never hated Fischer so much as I did then. He was taunting us both. He was taunting my disappointment and he was taunting the Divisionnaire's fear.

"At last you are facing the enemy's fire, Divisionnaire. Isn't it something you have dreamed about during all those long years of our Swiss neutrality?"

I heard the Divisionnaire's sad voice, while I stood staring at the dead and useless cracker in my hand.

"I was young then. I'm old now."

"But two million francs. I've known you a long time, Divisionnaire, and I know how much you value money. You married money, you certainly didn't marry beauty, but even when your wife died and left you all she had, it didn't satisfy you, or you wouldn't have come to my parties. Here's your chance. Two million francs which you will have won yourself. Two million francs for showing a little courage. Military courage. Facing fire, Divisionnaire."

I looked across the grass at the table and I saw that the old man was near to tears. I put my hand in the bran tub and pulled out the last cracker, the cracker which should have been Kips's. Again I tugged with my teeth and again there was the same small crack, no louder than a match striking.

"What a fool you are, Jones," Doctor Fischer said. "Where was the hurry? You've irritated me all the evening by your mere presence. You aren't like the others. You aren't in the picture. You haven't helped. You prove nothing. It isn't money you want. You are just greedy for death. I'm not interested in that sort of greed."

The Divisionnaire said, "But there's only my cracker left."

"Yes, Divisionnaire, and it's your turn now, all right. No getting out of it. You must play the game to the end. Get up. Put yourself at a safe distance. Unlike Jones, I don't want to die," but the old man didn't move.

"I can't shoot you for cowardice in the face of the enemy, but I can promise you the story will be all round Geneva."

I took the two checks out of the two cylinders and returned with them to the table. I tossed one of the checks to Fischer. "There's Mr. Kips's share," I said, "to divide among the others."

"You are keeping the other?"

"Yes."

He gave me one of his dangerous smiles. "After all, Jones, I have hopes of fitting you in the picture. Sit down and have another glass while the Divisionnaire picks up his courage. You are quite well off now. Relatively. In your own eyes. Draw the money out of the bank tomorrow and tuck it safely away, and I really believe that soon you will begin to feel like all the others. I might even start the parties again, if only to watch your greed growing. Mrs. Montgomery, Belmont, Kips, Deane, they were much like they are now when I first knew them. But I shall have created you. Just as much as God created Adam. Divisionnaire, your time's up. Don't keep us waiting any more. The party's over, the bonfires are going out, it's getting cold, and it's time for Albert to clear the table."

The Divisionnaire sat silent, his old head bowed toward the cracker on the table. I thought: He is really crying (I couldn't see his eyes), crying for the lost dream of heroism that I suppose every young soldier goes to bed with.

"Be a man, Divisionnaire."

"How you must despise yourself," I said to Doctor Fischer. I don't know what made me say those words. It was as though they had been whispered in my ear, and I had simply passed them on. I pushed the check down the table toward the Divisionnaire. I said, "I'll buy your cracker for two million francs. Give it me."

"No. No." He was hardly audible, but he didn't resist when I drew the cracker from his fingers.

"What do you mean, Jones?"

I couldn't bother to answer Doctor Fischer—I was on more important business—and anyway I didn't know the answer. The answer hadn't been given me by whoever had given me the words.

"Stop where you are, damn you. Tell me, what in Christ's name do you mean?"

I was far too happy to reply, for I had the Divisionnaire's cracker in my fingers and I walked away from the table down the slope of the lawn toward the lake, the direction which I had imagined Anna-Luise taking. The Divisionnaire buried his face in his hands as I passed; the gardeners had gone, and the bonfires were dying. "Come back," Doctor Fischer called after me, "come back, Jones. I want to talk to you."

I thought: When it comes to the point, he's afraid too. I suppose he wants to avoid a scandal. But I wasn't going to help him over that. This was a death which belonged to me, it was my child, my only child, and it was Anna-Luise's child too. No skiing accident could rob the two of us of the child I held in my hand. I wasn't lonely any longer— they were the lonely ones, the Divisionnaire and Doctor Fischer, sitting at opposite ends of the long table, waiting to hear the sound of my death.

I went down to the very edge of the lake, where the slope of the lawn would hide me from both of them, and for the third time, but this time with complete confidence, I took the tape between my teeth and pulled the cracker with my right hand.

The silly insignificant crack and the silence which followed told me how utterly I had been fooled. Doctor Fischer had stolen my death and humiliated the Divisionnaire; he had proved his point about the greed of his rich friends, and he was sitting at the table laughing at both of us. It had certainly been a good last party as far as he was concerned.

I couldn't hear his laughter at this distance. What I heard was the pad and the squeak of footsteps in the snow as they came along the edge of the lake. Whoever it was stopped abruptly when he saw me —all I could make out was a black suit against the white snow. I asked, "Who are you?"

"Why, it's Mr. Jones," a voice said. "Surely it's Mr. Jones."

"Yes."

"You've forgotten me. I'm Steiner."

"Why on earth are you here?"

"I couldn't stand it anymore."

"Stand what?"

"What he did to her."

At that moment my mind was occupied with Anna-Luise and I had no idea what he meant. Then I said, "There's nothing you can do about it now."

He said, "I heard about your wife. I am very sorry. She was so like Anna. When I heard she had died it was just as though Anna had died all over again. You must forgive me. I am talking clumsily."

"No. I can understand what you felt."

"Where is he?"

"If you mean Doctor Fischer, he's been playing his best and final joke and he's up there laughing to himself, I imagine."

"I've got to go and see him."

"What for?"

"When I was in that hospital I had a lot of time to think. It was seeing your wife which made me start to think. Seeing her in the shop was like Anna come alive. I had too much accepted things—he was so powerful—he had invented Dentophil Bouquet—he was a bit like God Almighty—he could take away my job—he could even take away Mozart. I never wanted to listen to Mozart after she died. You must understand, please, for her sake. We were never really lovers, but he made innocence dirty. Now I want to get near enough to him to spit in God Almighty's face."

"It's a bit too late for that, isn't it?"

"It's never too late to spit at God Almighty. He lasts forever and ever, amen. And he made us what we are."

"Perhaps he did, but Doctor Fischer didn't."

"He made me what I am now."

"Oh," I said—I was impatient with the little man who had broken my solitude—"go up there then and spit. A lot of good may it do you."

He looked away from me up the slope of the lawn which we could barely distinguish now in the dying light of the fires, but as it happened Mr.

Steiner didn't have to climb up the slope to find Doctor Fischer, for Doctor Fischer came climbing down to us, climbing slowly and laboriously, watching his own feet, which sometimes slid on an icy patch.

"Here he comes," I said, "so you had better get your spit ready."

We stood there waiting, and it seemed an interminable time before he reached us. He stopped a few feet away and said to me, "I didn't know you were here. I thought by this time you had probably gone away. They've all gone away. The Divisionnaire's gone."

"With his check?"

"Of course. With his check." He peered through the dark at my companion. He said, "You're not alone. Who is this man?"

"His name is Steiner."

"Steiner?" I had never before seen Doctor Fischer at a loss. It was as though he had left half his mind behind him at the table. He seemed to look toward me for help, but I gave him none.

"Who's Steiner? What's he doing here?" He had the air of searching a long time for something which he had mislaid, like a man turning over the objects in a cluttered drawer, seeking a checkbook or a passport.

"I knew your wife," Mr. Steiner said. "You made Mr. Kips dismiss me. You ruined both our lives."

After he had spoken the three of us stood there, silent in the darkness and the snow. It was as though we were all waiting for something to happen, but not one of us knew what it would be: a jeer, a blow, a simple turning away. It was the moment for Mr. Steiner to act, but he did nothing. Perhaps he knew his spit wouldn't carry far enough.

At last I said, "Your party was a great success."

"Yes?"

"You managed to humiliate us all. What are you going to do next?"

"I don't know."

Again I had the impression that he was looking to me for help. He said, "There was something you said just now . . ." It was incredible, the great Doctor Fischer of Geneva, looking to Alfred Jones to help him remember—what?

"How you must have laughed when I bought the last cracker, and you knew that all I would get was a little fart when I pulled it."

He said, "I didn't mean to humiliate *you*."

"It was an extra dividend for you, wasn't it?"

He said, "I hadn't planned it that way. You are not one of them," and he muttered their names: a sort of roll call of the Toads. "Kips, Deane, Mrs. Montgomery, the Divisionnaire, Belmont, and there were those two who died."

Mr. Steiner said, "You killed your wife."

"I didn't kill her."

"She died because she didn't want to live. Without love."

"Love? I don't read love stories, Steiner."

"But you love your money, don't you?"

"No. Jones will tell you tonight how I gave most of it away."

"What are you going to live for now, Fischer?" I asked. "I don't think any of your friends will come back."

Doctor Fischer said, "Are you so sure that I want to live? Do you want to live? You didn't seem to when you took those crackers. Does what's-his-name Steiner want to live? Yes, perhaps you both do. Perhaps when it comes to the point I have an inclination to live too. Or what am I doing standing here?"

"You had your fun tonight anyway," I said.

"Yes. It was better than nothing. Nothing is a bit frightening, Jones."

"It was a strange revenge you took," I said.

"What revenge?"

"All because one woman despised you, you had to despise all the world."

"She didn't despise me. Perhaps she hated me. No one will ever be able to despise me, Jones."

"Except yourself."

"Yes—I remember now that was what you said."

"It's true, isn't it?"

He said, "It was a disease I caught when you came into my life, Steiner. I should have told Kips to double your salary and I could have presented Anna with all the Mozart records she wanted. I could have bought you and her, like I bought all the others—except you, Jones. It's too late now to buy you. What *is* the time?"

"Past midnight," I said.

"Time to sleep."

He stood a moment in thought and then he set

off, but not in the direction of the house. He continued walking slowly along the lawn by the lakeside, until he was out of sight and sound in the silence of the snow. Even the waters of the lake didn't break the silence: there was no tide to lap on the shore below us.

"Poor man," Steiner said.

"You are very charitable, Mr. Steiner. I've never hated a man more."

"You hate him and I suppose I hate him too. But hate—it isn't important. Hate isn't contagious. It doesn't spread. One can hate one man and leave it there. But when you begin to despise like Doctor Fischer, you end by despising all the world."

"I wish you had done what you planned and spat in his face."

"I couldn't. You see—when it came to the point —I pitied him."

How I wished Fischer had been there to hear how he was pitied by Mr. Steiner.

"It's too cold standing around," I said, "we'll catch our death. . . ." But wasn't that, I thought, what I wanted to do? If I stayed long enough. A sharp sound tore the thought in two.

"What was that?" Steiner said. "A car backfiring?"

"We are too far from the road for that."

We only had to walk a hundred yards before we came on Doctor Fischer's body. The revolver which he must have carried in his pocket lay beside his head. The snow was already absorbing the blood. I put out my hand to take the gun—it might, I thought, serve my turn too—but Mr. Steiner stopped me. "Leave that to the police," he said. I looked at the body and it had no more significance than a dead dog. This, I thought, was the bit of rubbish I had once compared in my mind with Jehovah and Satan.

17

The fact that I have written this narrative tells well
enough that, unlike Doctor Fischer, I never found
the courage necessary to kill myself; that night I
hadn't needed courage, for I had a sufficiency of
despair, but since the inquest demonstrated that
the revolver had contained only one charge, my
despair would not have served me even if Mr. Steiner had not taken possession of the weapon. Courage is sapped by day-to-day mind-dulling routine,
and despair deepens so much every day one lives,
that death seems in the end to lose its point. I had
felt Anna-Luise close to me when I held the whisky
in my hand and again when I pulled the cracker
with my teeth, but now I had lost all hope of ever
seeing her in any future. Only if I had believed in
a God could I have dreamed that the two of us
would ever have that *jour le plus long*. It was as
though my small half-belief had somehow shri-

veled with the sight of Doctor Fischer's body. Evil
was as dead as a dog, and why should goodness
have more immortality than evil? There was no
longer any reason to follow Anna-Luise if it was
only into nothingness. As long as I lived, I could at
least remember her. I had two snapshots of her
and a note in her hand written to make an appointment before we lived together; there was the chair
which she used to sit in, and the kitchen where she
had jangled the plates before we bought the ma-
chine. All these were like the relics of bone they
keep in Roman Catholic churches. Once as I boiled
myself an egg for my supper, I heard myself repeating a line which I had heard spoken by a priest
at the midnight Mass at Saint Maurice: "As often as
you do these things you shall do them in memory
of me." Death was no longer an answer—it was an
irrelevance.

Sometimes I have a cup of coffee with Mr. Steiner—he isn't a drinking man. He talks of Anna-
Luise's mother and I don't interrupt him. I let him
ramble on and I think of Anna-Luise. Our enemy
is dead and our hate has died with him, and we are
left with our two very different memories of love.
The Toads still live in Geneva and I go to that city
as seldom as I can. Once near the station I saw
Belmont, but we didn't speak. I have passed Mr.
Kips several times too, but he doesn't see me with
his gaze fixed on the pavement, and the only time
I encountered Deane he was far too drunk to notice me. Only Mrs. Montgomery once troubled me
in Geneva, calling cheerfully from the doorway of

a jeweler's shop, "Why, if it isn't Mr. Smith," but I pretended not to hear and hurried on to meet an Argentinian client.